COLD CASE TRUE CRIME

———

Denise N. Wheatley

To my mother, who's the most glamorous bookworm I know.
Thank you for introducing me to the wonderful world of
Harlequin all those years ago.

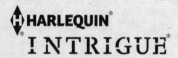

ISBN-13: 978-1-335-48900-5

Cold Case True Crime

Copyright © 2021 by Denise N. Wheatley

This edition published by arrangement with Harlequin Books S.A.

For questions and comments about the quality of this book,
please contact us at CustomerService@Harlequin.com.

Harlequin Enterprises ULC
22 Adelaide St. West, 40th Floor
Toronto, Ontario M5H 4E3, Canada
www.Harlequin.com

Printed in U.S.A.

"Hello?" the detective said after answering on the first ring. Samantha was surprised to hear that he sounded wide-awake.

"Detective Har—I mean, Gregory?"

"Yeah, hey. How ironic that you'd be calling me at this ungodly hour. I was actually just thinking about you."

"Were you?" Samantha asked, momentarily forgetting all about her home being vandalized. "What were you thinking about?"

"I just finished reading your latest blog post about Jacob. This is great stuff, Sam. I mean, you did go in on Collin pretty hard, but you presented some solid evidence that backs up your claims. And I love the way you concluded the post. 'Come on, people,'" he read. "'Do the right thing. Come forward. Speak up. Be heard. Help bring justice to Jacob Jennings and his family. Because as we all know, someone knows something...' That's really awesome, the way you worded that ending."

"Thanks, Gregory. Unfortunately, the post really struck a nerve in a certain someone here in Gattenburg."

"What, did you receive some negative feedback on it?"

"Worse. My house was just vandalized."

Denise N. Wheatley loves happy endings and the art of storytelling. Her novels run the romance gamut, and she strives to pen entertaining books that embody matters of the heart. She's an RWA member and holds a BA in English from the University of Illinois. When Denise isn't writing, she enjoys watching true crime TV and chatting with readers. Follow her on social media.

Instagram: @Denise_Wheatley_Writer
Twitter: @DeniseWheatley
BookBub: @DeniseNWheatley
Goodreads: Denise N. Wheatley

Books by Denise N. Wheatley

Harlequin Intrigue

Cold Case True Crime

Visit the Author Profile page at Harlequin.com.

CAST OF CHARACTERS

Samantha Vincent—A popular true-crime cold-case blogger who's determined to uncover the truth behind an old friend's murder.

Gregory Harris—A devoted police detective who's torn between joining forces with Samantha in the pursuit of justice and remaining loyal to his brothers in blue.

Ava Jennings—Samantha's friend who turns to the blogger for help in solving her brother's mysterious death.

Jacob Jennings—Ava's dead brother, whose body was found near Westman's Automotive Factory, where he worked as a team assembler.

Collin Wentworth—A known troublemaker who was Jacob's childhood friend. He currently manages Westman's Automotive.

Walter Wentworth—The chief of police in Gattenburg, Illinois, and Collin's father.

Kenzie Stevenson—Jacob's coworker at Westman's, Collin's ex-girlfriend and an anonymous source for Samantha.

Victor Elliot—Gattenburg's well-respected mayor.

Hudson Taylor—Another coworker of Jacob's and an anonymous source for Samantha.

Axel Guzman—A well-known member of the Midwest drug cartel.

Chapter One

Samantha Vincent flinched when the coffee shop door slammed shut behind her. She stared down the dark, vacant street in search of her car—she hadn't realized she'd parked so far away.

The temperature had dropped severely since she'd arrived at the café. There was now a stinging chill in the night air. She set out toward the sidewalk, tightening her houndstooth-patterned scarf in an effort to block the wind as it whistled eerily past her ears.

Samantha had spent the day working on her popular true crime cold case blog, *Someone Knows Something*, and time had gotten away from her. By now, businesses were closed and most residents of small-town Gattenburg, Illinois, had retired for the evening.

A frigid breeze whipped through her golden-brown bob and blew open Samantha's black wool peacoat, sending unsettling shivers throughout her entire body. But it wasn't just the icy climate that had unnerved her.

She was still rattled by an email she'd received from Ava Jennings, an old high school friend whose family Samantha had grown close to after spending countless days at their home during her teenage years. In her message, Ava pleaded with Samantha to investigate her brother Jacob's mysterious death, which police had just officially stated was cold with no leads.

Tree branches scraped against dim streetlights that barely illuminated the road. Samantha glanced down at the ground, her lone shadow a stark reminder that she was unaccompanied in the unnerving darkness. Moments like these brought on paranoid thoughts of all the unsolved cases she worked so hard to crack. Many of those victims found themselves in her exact same position seconds before their demise—isolated and vulnerable.

Samantha pushed those disturbing thoughts out of her mind and hurried along the pavement. Her feet ached in her high-heeled boots. But in spite of the pain, she clenched her jaw and fought through it, anxious to get off the desolate street and inside her car.

Just when Samantha's convertible appeared in the hazy distance, the sound of screeching tires pierced her eardrums.

She stopped abruptly. The vehicle's engine emitted a menacing roar.

Samantha spun around, almost losing her footing. Bright yellow headlights blinded her squinted chestnut eyes. She inhaled sharply, watching while the black sedan crept toward her.

She curled her hands into tight fists and took a step back, her lean legs quivering in the wind. Remembering the mini stun gun she'd slipped into her back pocket, Samantha pulled it out and contemplated making a run for her car. But she was too afraid to turn her back on the man she presumed was behind the wheel.

Collin Wentworth...

That's the name Ava had mentioned several times

throughout her email as she dissected the details of her brother's murder.

Collin and Jacob had been childhood friends who grew apart during their teenage years once Collin went rogue. The incident that officially ended their friendship occurred one night when Collin convinced Jacob to accompany him on a wild joyride in a stolen vehicle. After being apprehended by the police, Jacob received six months in a juvenile detention center while Collin was given probation. That's when Jacob realized it was time for them to go their separate ways. But the pair remained cordial over the years, and Collin even hired Jacob to work for him at Westman's Automotive Factory, where Jacob served as a team assembler building car engines and Collin acted as the facility's general manager.

The day Jacob's body was found, he'd met with Collin to discuss the whereabouts of three fellow team assemblers who had gone missing. The official police report noted that Jacob had been seen walking out of the factory with Collin while having what appeared to be a heated conversation. After a brief exchange, they went their separate ways. Collin admitted to police that he'd spoken with Jacob the day he went missing. But he refused to disclose the details of their conversation. Ava believed that Collin was the last person to see Jacob alive.

Collin was a narcissist whose temper exploded when he drank. From bar fights to the destruction of property, public intoxication to reckless driving, his foul reputation certainly preceded him. But because Collin's father was Walter Wentworth, Gattenburg's chief of police, he usually got off with light warnings and slaps on the wrist.

Ava was convinced that Collin was withholding information that could help solve the case.

Beep, beep!

Samantha jumped at the sound of the blaring horn. The looming car was getting closer. She couldn't help but wonder whether Collin had seen her latest blog post, where she'd insisted that he could've been a huge help in Jacob's death investigation had he simply cooperated with the police.

News tended to spread quickly throughout Gattenburg, and Collin seemed to have undercover eyes and ears all over town.

Samantha shoved her trembling fingers inside her handbag in search of her key fob. When sharp metal edges grazed her palm, she grabbed it and pounded the remote until her taillights blinked up ahead.

Her calf muscles throbbed as she sprinted into the street. The second she grasped her door handle, screeching brakes brought the menacing car to a halt right next to her. She tightened the grip on her stun gun, watching through the corner of her eye as the tinted passenger window lowered.

"I thought that was you…" a low voice boomed.

Samantha's heart thumped erratically at the thought of coming face-to-face with Collin. She bent down and peered inside the car.

When she locked eyes with Gregory Harris, a handsome police detective who was new to Gattenburg, Samantha inhaled sharply.

"Officer Harris!" she exclaimed, gripping her chest

with relief. "Hello. Hi. I, uh—sorry. I thought you were someone else."

He chuckled softly, his full, sexy lips spreading into a crooked grin. "Really? Well, I hope you're not too disappointed that it's just me."

"No," she murmured, reaching back and discreetly slipping her stun gun into her pocket. "Not at all."

A jolt of heat shot up Samantha's spine. The detective had had that effect on her ever since she met him last month at Hannah's Coffee Shop.

He had just moved to Gattenburg from Chicago, where he'd worked on the police force for over ten years. Detective Harris claimed to have left in search of a slower, more peaceful lifestyle. But the bitterness behind his dark brown eyes told a different story when he spoke of his departure.

The detective reached out and turned down the radio, his muscular arm bulging through his navy cashmere sweater. "I'm guessing you just left the coffee shop after working on your blog all day?"

"You guessed right. I usually don't stay this late, but I was on a roll."

"Wow. Your dedication to reporting on all those mysterious cold cases is admirable. That piece you wrote last week about the kidnapped student at the University of Illinois? Impressive."

Samantha's skin tingled under his intense stare. "Why, thank you. I appreciate that."

"You're welcome. So, what's the latest post about?"

She paused, her cheerful expression wilting into one of concern.

"The death of an old high school friend." Samantha's voice quaked. She cleared her throat before continuing.

"His name was Jacob Jennings. You may have heard of him. He died mysteriously months ago, and his body was found two blocks away from Westman's Automotive Factory."

"Hmm," the detective sighed, running his large hand over his freshly trimmed goatee. "That name doesn't ring a bell."

Samantha dropped her head in disappointment. "Of course it doesn't. The case went cold less than forty-eight hours into the investigation. The Gattenburg Police Department has done nothing to solve it. That's why I've committed to helping Jacob's sister get to the bottom of it. And I'll be using *Someone Knows Something* to provide the community with updates on my progress. If I can stir up some sort of public outcry, maybe the police department will feel pressured to reopen the case."

She hesitated, waiting to hear Gregory's response. When he shifted in his seat and remained silent, she pressed on.

"Hey, I'd love to get your take on the situation. The fact that you're new to the Gattenburg PD is huge. You'd bring a fresh eye to the investigation. Plus you've got access to the file and critical inside information. If we join forces, I bet you and I could—"

Detective Harris held up his hand. "Hold on, Samantha. First off, let me just say that I am very sorry to hear about the loss of your friend. With that being said, I'm new to this force, and there are certain protocols that I need to follow. I know I haven't been in Gattenburg for very long, but judging from the upstanding reputation and track record of Chief Wentworth, I can't imagine he didn't do all that he could to ensure Jacob's death was thoroughly investigated."

Despite the gust of cold air that swept past Samantha, she felt herself growing hot with frustration. She loosened her scarf and took a deep breath.

"Detective Harris, there is so much more to this case than you know. And if I may be blunt, there are rumors that some of the men in blue working next to you aren't as ethical as they may seem."

An uneasy silence filled the air. Samantha crossed her arms and tapped her foot rapidly against the asphalt. She knew she was being forward, but after hearing that a new detective would be joining the force, she'd hoped there would be renewed interest in the investigation, along with a fresh perspective.

After several tense seconds, the detective finally spoke up.

"Listen. The reason I'm no longer with the Chicago PD is because I refused to abide by the department's shady code of silence. So if I suspected there was any corruption going on within Gattenburg's law enforcement agency, believe me, I'd be the first one to call it out."

Samantha resisted the urge to slam her fist against the hood of his car. "Says the man who joined the force literally a month ago…"

"Wow. Okay," Gregory sighed, running his hand down his thick, closely cropped black hair. "Samantha, I understand that you and your friend are hurting. But please know that this force's only objective is to do the right thing. I may be new, but I've had connections here in Gattenburg for years. And I don't believe there are any cover-ups happening. So, with that being said, maybe we should end this conversation before it goes too far—"

"Fine," Samantha interrupted, taking a step back. "And with all due respect, Officer Harris, I think you're being a bit naive. If nothing else, I do hope you'll continue following my blog. It'll open your eyes to the truth. And with *that* being said, have a good night."

Before the detective could respond, Samantha climbed inside her car and sped off.

GREGORY FELT A pull in his chest as he watched Samantha drive away. Bumping into her had been such a pleasant surprise. He'd barely been able to control the shudders of excitement in his gut during their conversation. But that buzz completely fizzled after their encounter ended in disaster.

He drove somberly down the street before noticing Samantha stopped at a red light up ahead. The detective quickly maneuvered his car alongside hers and rolled down the window.

When he glanced over, he noticed tears trickling down her cheeks.

"Hey! Sam!" he called out, frantically waving his arms.

She stared straight ahead. As soon as the light turned green, she jetted off.

Gregory hit the accelerator and followed her. Before he knew it, he'd trailed her all the way home. When she noticed him parked in front of her house, she stormed over to his car.

"Here we go…" he muttered, opening the door and stepping out.

"What are you doing?" Samantha snapped. "Did you really just follow me home?"

"I did. I, uh… I wanted to apologize for the way I

responded to you." He tried to ignore the rush of energy he felt at the sight of her curls blowing seductively across her delicate face.

Focus, he thought, shoving his hands deep inside his pockets.

"I know that losing a friend so tragically can't be easy," he continued, "and I hope I didn't seem insensitive. I'm just very protective of my brothers in blue. But I should've been more sympathetic toward you."

"Humph," Samantha huffed, tilting her head to the side and studying him closely. "Well…thank you for that. I accept your apology."

Gregory felt his taut muscles relax when he sensed that she had dropped her guard a bit.

She shook her head and stared up at the sky. "This all just feels so surreal. I'm not used to covering cases that hit so close to home. And the fact that this one hasn't been solved really hurts. It actually makes me wish I would've followed in my father's footsteps and gone into law enforcement. But that didn't end well."

"What do you mean?" he asked.

"My dad was killed in the line of duty back in Chicago. The fire went out of my desire to join the force after that."

Gregory moved in closer and gently placed his hand on Samantha's arm. "I'm so sorry. I didn't realize your father died on the job."

"That's what brought my mom and me here to Gattenburg. We needed a fresh start in what we thought would be a safe town. And now this. Which is why I can't just stand by and do nothing. I went through that once with my dad's killer. I refuse to go through it again."

"Wait, what do you mean? Your father's murderer wasn't apprehended?"

"No." Samantha sighed, dabbing her fingertips against the corners of her damp eyes. "The offender was a big-time drug dealer who'd been paying off several city officials. Apparently that dirty money meant more to them than justice for my father."

"You certainly have my sympathies, Samantha. But when it comes to Jacob's case, I'd be remiss if I didn't advise you to use caution."

"Why?"

The detective hesitated, struggling to choose his words wisely. "I'll put it this way. Chief Wentworth and Gattenburg's judicial powers that be have a very... *amiable* relationship. They make special efforts to look out for one another. And while I now know that the investigation into Jacob's death concluded somewhat hastily—"

"Somewhat," Samantha interjected.

"—it could in fact be because Collin is Chief Wentworth's son," Gregory continued, purposely ignoring her sarcasm. "And I'm not saying that Collin was involved, because that I don't know. I'm just going off what you're telling me. But what I *do* know is that Chief Wentworth is a trusted leader in this community. As far as the higher-ups are concerned, he can do no wrong. And while I do respect the chief, I'll admit he can be one relentless son of a bitch."

Samantha backed away from him. "I'm not afraid of the chief! He may have a hold on this town, and he's clearly got all of you under his spell. But he's got nothing on me."

"I'm not saying you should be afraid," Gregory lamented. "Just be careful."

When Samantha waved him off, he pressed on.

"Listen to me. Chief Wentworth has a lot of power. And when it comes to his son, he does appear to be jaded. If you even insinuate that Collin's involved some sort of illegal activity, the chief could see to it that Jacob's case is never reopened."

Samantha threw her arms out at her sides. "It shouldn't matter *who's* involved in Jacob's death. The bottom line is he deserves a proper investigation. And that starts with Chief Wentworth putting an end to the nepotism and doing his job. He should want to get Jacob's killer off the street, even if it is his own son. Now, if you're not with me, then you're against me. So thanks for letting me know where you stand. We're done here."

She spun around and stormed up her walkway.

"I'm not against you, Samantha!" Gregory called out. "It's just that…" His voice faded as the sting of remorse burned his throat.

He waited until she was safely inside the house before hopping in his car and speeding off, anxious to get home and check her blog to find out what she'd reported on Jacob's case thus far.

Chapter Two

And that, my dear readers, Samantha typed, is how you color code your calendar in order to remain organized throughout the week.

She saved the document to her *Elevate Women's Journal* file, then glanced around the dining area of Danica's Deli.

The afternoon crowd had already cleared out of the quaint 1950s-style eatery. Most of the red vinyl booths and high-top tables were empty. A few patrons still sat in swivel stools along the counter, chatting up the servers while finishing their meals.

Samantha's head was still buzzing after meeting with Ava for lunch a couple of hours ago. She couldn't wait to post the latest intel she'd just received on Jacob's murder.

Before she was able to get to that, Samantha had to edit her monthly "A Woman's Guide to Practical Living" column for the women's journal, which was what paid the bills.

Just as she began composing an email to her column's editor, Regina, her cell phone buzzed.

"Speaking of the devil," she moaned after glancing

down and seeing a text message notification from Regina pop up on the screen.

Samantha rushed to email the article to her, then opened the text.

Hey, Sam! Please be sure to turn your column in to me before 3:00 p.m. I'd like to finalize the layout by tomorrow so that we can go to press before the end of the week.
Thanks! Regina

"Two steps ahead of ya, Reggie Reg," Samantha muttered as she replied to the message.

Good afternoon! Have you checked your email recently? I just sent the article to you. Looking forward to hearing your thoughts. Thank you!

As soon as she sent the text, Samantha felt a strong, warm hand grip her shoulder. She gasped and practically jumped out of her seat before grabbing the edge of the table and spinning around.

When she saw Detective Harris standing over her, Samantha closed her eyes and emitted a slow sigh of relief.

"Hey, you," he chuckled, clearly amused by her startled reaction. "I didn't scare you, did I?"

"Um, *yeah*, you did."

In spite of still being irritated with him for refusing to get involved with the investigation of Jacob's death, Samantha felt her demeanor soften at the sight of the detective's seductive smirk.

"You can't just walk up on somebody like that from

behind and put your hands on them," she continued, her high-pitched tone filled with sass.

"My apologies. Next time I'll be sure to walk up on you from the front before I put my hands on you…"

Samantha eyed the detective curiously, taken aback by his blatant flirtation.

"So what's up?" he asked, glancing over at her computer screen. "You working on your blog?"

"Not yet. I just wrote an article for the women's journal I work for called *Elevate*. Now that it's done, I'll be getting back to *Someone Knows Something*."

As Detective Harris's gaze traveled from Samantha's eyes to her lips and lingered there, she felt flickers of heat creep up the back of her neck. She grabbed her glass of iced green tea and took several long sips.

"I checked out your blog when I got home last night. After our—" he paused, staring up at the ceiling as if searching for the right words to say "—rather *spirited* conversation, I decided to look a little deeper into Jacob's death. But I noticed you hadn't posted much information on it."

"That's because I didn't have much information on it up until now. I just had lunch with his sister, Ava, and she shared a ton of info with me."

Samantha paused, peering at the detective as he appeared to hang on her every word.

"Wait." She continued, "What's with the sudden curiosity? I thought you weren't interested in finding out the truth about Jacob's murder."

Detective Harris turned away from her. He shifted his weight from one foot to the other, then shrugged his shoulders.

"I was never *not* interested. You've just managed to capture my attention."

Samantha couldn't tell whether he was referring to her blog, or her, or both. Either way, his suggestive statement caused a tingling sensation to swirl inside her chest.

"Oh, so I've captured your attention, huh?" she quipped.

"Yes. You have. And don't be shocked by what I'm about to say, but I'd actually like to check out the area where Jacob's body was found."

She leaned back in her chair as her eyelids lowered with surprise. "Really? *Wow.* I am shocked to hear that. And what's interesting is that after meeting with Ava today, I was thinking I should go check out the crime scene as well. Maybe even post some photos of it on *Someone Knows Something.* You never know. Those pics might trigger someone to come forward with information on something they've seen or heard."

The detective glanced down at his watch. The corners of his shapely lips curled into a subtle smile.

Just as thoughts of how his mouth would feel pressed against hers crept into Samantha's mind, he spoke up.

"Well, what do you think of us heading over there together now?" he asked before abruptly holding out his hands. "I mean, unless you're too busy and don't have time."

"No, no. Now is cool, actually. That way I can get those photos taken and include them in my next blog post. Plus this will give me a chance to tell you everything I found out from Ava today. If you want to hear about it, that is," she added quickly.

Samantha folded her hands tightly, anxiously awaiting his response. It was clear that she and the detective were both walking on eggshells with one another as they wondered just how far this investigation would take them. She hoped that this would be the start of his involvement in the cold case.

"Sure," he said, readjusting the shoulder holster that was tucked inside his black leather bomber jacket. "I'm open to hearing more about it. Did you drive here?"

"I did. I'm assuming you did as well?"

"Yes. Why don't you leave your car here and I'll drive?"

The thought of sitting in the car next to Detective Harris caused a wave of nervous flutters in the pit of Samantha's stomach.

Okay, she thought to herself. *Stop acting like a googly-eyed high schooler and pull yourself together.*

"Yes, that does make sense," she said, struggling not to sound as excited as she felt.

Samantha looked down and noticed that her hands were shaking as she closed her laptop and slid her things inside her tote bag. She peeked over at the detective, hoping he wasn't watching her fumble about. Luckily he was too busy tapping away on his cell phone to notice.

After taking a few discreet, calming breaths, Samantha drained her glass of iced tea, stood up and grabbed her bag.

"Are you ready?" she asked. *"Partner?"*

"Hold on, now, hold on," Detective Harris chuckled. "Don't go getting too excited. Just because I'm accompanying you to the crime scene doesn't mean I'm about to get all wrapped up in this case with you."

"We'll see," she rebutted.

And with that, Samantha spun around on her heels,

brushing up against the detective's gym-honed chest before sashaying toward the door with an extra twist in her hips.

GREGORY SWALLOWED HARD, struggling to compose himself. He couldn't take his eyes off Samantha as she breezed past him. Her slim, curvy silhouette, which was perfectly outlined in her cropped moto jacket and dark blue skinny jeans, roused a sensation within him that he hadn't felt in quite some time.

"You coming?" Samantha asked him, her hair swinging over her shoulder when she turned around and peered back at him.

He put a little pep in his step and hurried toward the door.

"Yep, I'm right behind you."

Pull it together, man…

Gregory held the door open for Samantha, then shuffled over to her right side, making sure that she walked on the inside of the sidewalk.

"Such a gentleman," she gushed. "Thank you."

He glanced over at her, wondering whether her flirty demeanor was genuine or if she was putting on a show in an effort to lure him further into her investigation. Either way, he liked it.

"I'm parked right up ahead, on the corner," Gregory told her while pointing at a black Chevy sedan with black tinted windows.

"Nice. This makes me feel like I'm going on a real-life ride along."

"Uh-oh," he chuckled, amused by her excitement as she practically skipped toward the car and grabbed the passenger door handle.

Gregory clicked the key fob. When the doors un-locked, he moved in a bit closer than necessary and gently placed his hand over hers. "Here, let me get that for you."

Samantha looked up at Gregory and emitted a slight gasp. The pair stood so close to one another that he could smell the piece of cinnamon candy rolling around in her mouth.

"Thanks," she said quietly, taking a step back.

Gregory opened the door and once again found his eyes stuck on Samantha, watching while she slipped inside the car. She looked up at him and opened her mouth, as if she were going to say something. But then she turned and looked straight ahead, remaining silent.

The detective would've been confused had it not been for the glimmer in her eyes. He'd seen that twin-kle time and time again while on the force, in the gaze of many people he'd encountered over the years. By now he knew that it was an indication of pure gratitude for listening, for taking them seriously.

He jogged around to the driver's side, patting his jacket just to make sure the report he'd copied before leaving the station was still securely tucked away in-side his pocket. It was.

Gregory hadn't yet told Samantha that he'd pulled Jacob's file and studied up on his case. He didn't know how deeply involved he wanted to get just yet. The de-tective figured he'd see how today went, then decide from there.

"So the location where Jacob's body was found isn't too far from here," he told her after climbing inside the car and pulling off.

"Not at all. According to the map app on my phone, the exact address is less than three miles away."

"Right. So Westman's Automotive Factory is on Everhart Avenue, and Jacob's body was recovered in an alleyway off Kenwood Street."

"Correct," Samantha confirmed. "And Kenwood is located two blocks away from Westman's, which you already know is where Jacob worked."

Gregory noticed a change in her demeanor. She was sitting straight up in her seat, her expression stern as she typed away on her cell phone.

Gone was the coy, playful attitude she'd had back at the deli. She was now strictly business. Had he not known any better, Samantha's authoritative attitude would've had him thinking she was a member of law enforcement. But then he remembered that her father had been a police officer, and he assumed she'd acquired some of that commanding bravado from him.

The detective glanced down at her slender left hand, which was perfectly manicured with pale pink nail polish. She wore a silver band on her pinkie finger, but her ring finger was noticeably bare.

What are you doing? he asked himself.

Gregory never paid attention to those types of minor details, especially when it came to a woman's marital status.

Stay focused...

"So according to Ava," Samantha continued, "the alleyway where Jacob was found is on the eight hundred block of Kenwood."

"Yes. Near housing numbers eight fifteen and eight seventeen, to be exact. I saw that his body was discovered in between two large metal dumpsters. And honestly, after seeing the crime scene photos, it looked to me as though his body had been forced into that small space. There's no way he could've ended up there on his own, especially if he was high on drugs like the police report suggested, and…"

Gregory's voice trailed off when he noticed Samantha gripping her chest while scrutinizing him intently.

"After seeing the crime scene photos?" she repeated. "And like the police report suggested? Umph. Sounds to me like you've done your homework on this case. I thought you weren't interested in getting involved. What's with the sudden change of heart?"

There's a beautiful, intelligent, inquisitive woman who cares about this deceased individual and who's captured my attention, he wanted to blurt out. But instead, the detective kept his cool and racked his brain for a more appropriate answer.

"Well," he began right before stopping at a red light and turning to her, "after that heated exchange we had in front of your house, you sparked my curiosity. Your pain over Jacob's death and desire to see him get the proper justice pushed me to take a look at the police report and find out what took place during the investigation."

"I appreciate that," Samantha uttered, crossing her arms and staring out the window. She eyed the quaint Tudor-style homes and their perfectly manicured lawns lining the narrow street, while struggling to keep her cool. "I'm sure it didn't take long for you to realize just how botched, rushed and inadequate that investigation was. I mean, seriously, it was a complete sham. I'd love to see that police report. It's probably one tiny little paragraph long. Tops."

Gregory once again held his hand to his pocket and discreetly tucked the police report farther inside. No matter how involved he got with Samantha and this case, he had no plans of going against department policy and disclosing any of the investigation's confidential details. At least that was his intention...

"So tell me more about your meeting with Ava," the detective said as he made a right turn onto Everhart Avenue. The bleak, desolate street, which was where Westman's Automotive Factory was located, was a drastic switch from the charming areas surrounding it. "You said you found out a lot more about Jacob's death than you knew before. What'd you learn?"

"Well, we already knew this but, we talked about the medical examiner's ruling that Jacob's death was an accidental drug overdose. That's a huge red flag in the case."

"Okay, and why is that a red flag?"

Gregory noticed Samantha slump down in her seat as they drove past Westman's, which took up half the block. Her eyes filled with tears as she peered out at the industrial building's drab gray cement exterior. It was clear that the owners hadn't done much to maintain the factory's appearance since it had been built in the 1960s. Its few dark windows were covered in thick layers of dust. Old, rusted auto parts had been carelessly tossed along the side of the discolored outer wall. Overgrown patches of grass blew against the crumbling facade.

"Wow," she sighed. "This place just reeks of depression. There's something sinister about it." She shook her head and turned away. "Anyway, the idea of Jacob overdosing on drugs is asinine. He's never done drugs a day in his life. And trust me, he liked to party back in the day. He could drink anybody in this town under the table. But drugs? That's never been Jacob's thing."

"Hmm," the detective breathed thoughtfully while making a left turn down Kenwood Street. "That's interesting. I did a little research on Westman's and saw that they have a pretty strong support system for former drug addicts."

"Yeah. Ava mentioned that, too. Before Jacob died, he talked up the company's bid to help recovering addicts get back on their feet by giving employment opportunities to people with felony drug convictions."

Gregory pulled his car into the alleyway where Jacob's body had been found and let up on the accelerator. "True. But before the employees could gain permanent employment, they had to complete a one-week second-chance program. If they didn't get through that and pass random drug tests during their three-month probationary period, then they weren't officially hired."

"Please." Samantha snorted as the detective crept toward a pair of rusted-out green metal dumpsters. "Do you really believe that?"

"Yes. I do. Westman's has been applauded by the entire community of Gattenburg for their efforts to help recovering addicts stay clean and obtain job opportunities. The mayor even honored the factory's efforts last month with a community impact award."

Samantha slid toward the edge of her seat and pointed up ahead. "It looks like those dumpsters are the only two in the alley. This must be the crime scene."

Gregory craned his neck and eyed the entire length of the passage. "I think you're right." He parked the car off to the side near a garage door. "Let's hop out and take a closer look."

A chill swept through Samantha as she opened the camera app on her cell phone. She stepped out of the car and took several pictures of the waste containers, moving back and forth in an effort to capture every angle.

"So wait a minute," she said, bending down and shuffling in closer. "Jacob's body was found in this tight little space in between these two dumpsters?"

"From the looks of the crime scene photos, yes."

While Samantha examined the cement walls located on either side of the bins, Gregory found himself once again unable to tear his gaze away from her long, lean legs.

She placed her hand on her curvy hip and tilted her head to the side.

"Judging from the snug proximity of the dumpsters to these walls," Samantha continued, "there's no room for them to be moved farther apart. So I agree with you in that Jacob had to have been shoved in between this space by somebody else. There's no way he could've ended up here on his own. Especially if he was high on drugs, as law enforcement would like for us to believe."

Just as Samantha began taking close-up photographs of the area, a loud engine roared down at the end of the alleyway. She and Gregory simultaneously jerked their heads toward the thunderous rumble.

"What the…" the detective uttered.

He stood up and tried to get a better look at the vehicle. But before he could catch a real glimpse, its tires screeched and skidded down the block.

"Got it," Samantha said while staring down at her cell phone.

"Got what?"

"A few pics of that vehicle. Looks like it was a white

van with some sort of blue and orange signage along the side."

"Hmm," Gregory grunted. "Interesting. Sounds like it may have been some sort of business vehicle, then?"

Samantha stared up at him, nodding her head knowingly while holding up her phone. "The photos are a bit blurry. But if I'm not mistaken, I spy an orange letter *R* and a blue letter *Y.* Wanna take a wild guess as to what company in Gattenburg has blue and orange signage on their white vans, with that lettering in their name?"

Gregory took the phone and scrolled through the fuzzy images.

"Westman's Automotive Factory," Samantha blurted out before giving him a chance to respond. "Do you see it?" she asked, frantically tapping her fingertip against the phone screen. "Right there. Can you make it out? Because I can."

"Yeah, you're right," Gregory replied smoothly in an effort to keep her calm. He could tell by the shrill tone of her voice that she was getting worked up.

Samantha threw her arms out to her sides and kicked up a few rocks with her black ankle boot. "Good to know that it's not just me. You see what I see."

"No, it's not just you." The detective scrolled back to the clearest photo and enlarged it. "I definitely see the end of Westman's company name here." An uneasy twinge pulled inside his chest. "Hey, would you mind texting those photos to me?"

"Of course not." Samantha took the phone and pulled up his name in her list of contacts. "It looks like the only number I have saved for you is your work phone down at the station."

"Really? I could've sworn I'd given you my personal

cell the night we ran into one another at the community center fundraiser."

"Nope," she chirped. "You didn't."

He held out his hand. "Here, let me program it in for you. I'll give you my personal email address, too."

Samantha handed him the phone, her eyebrows rising curiously.

"You know," Gregory quickly added, "in the event that you ever need to send me something."

"Mmm-hmm," she muttered, her tone filled with skepticism. It seemed clear to her that the detective was slowly getting more involved in Jacob's case than he'd initially intended. "Well, I appreciate that. From the looks of things," she continued, pointing toward the alleyway entrance where the Westman's van had appeared, "I just may be needing you."

Gregory stopped typing his email address into the phone and glanced up at her, wondering whether she was referring to more than just the investigation. He couldn't quite tell from the tense, faraway look in her eyes.

"So," Samantha continued, "don't you find it odd that the factory's vehicle was creeping past the crime scene like that? Then the driver revved its engine like a complete maniac once he saw us?"

"I don't know," he said, not wanting to make her fearful. "The factory is located a couple of blocks away from here. So the drive-by could've simply been a coincidence."

Samantha crossed her arms tightly in front of her. "Nah, I'm not going for that. I think there's more to it. And you know what they say—criminals love returning to the scene of the crime."

Gregory saved his information in Samantha's phone and handed it back to her. "That is what they say. But when it comes to this case, I don't want to jump to any unsubstantiated conclusions."

She twisted her lips warily. "Come on. Seriously? That was no coincidence. But anyway, I'm texting the photos to you now. I can't wait to show these to Ava and tell her about how you and I came out here and—"

"Hey," Gregory interrupted, holding out his hand. "Let me say this. I'm not trying to control whom you discuss your personal investigation into this case with or anything. But I'd like for you to refrain from telling anyone you've been talking about it with me. You know I'm new on the force, and I'm all about following the proper code of police conduct."

"Okay," Samantha replied coolly, shrugging her shoulders as if the request didn't bother her.

But when the detective noticed her pink-glossed lips turn downward, he knew that it had.

"Look, I hope you can understand why I don't want you to—"

"I do," she interjected before he could finish. "So no worries. I get it."

Gregory turned around and eyed the alleyway entrance again. "Well, now that we've both gotten a look at the crime scene and you've taken your photos, we should probably get out of here."

"Good idea. I don't want to be here if that van comes back around. Thanks for bringing me along to check it out. Between my meeting with Ava and these pics, I've got some great new leads to post on *Someone Knows Something.*"

"No problem. Glad you were able to join me."

The pair climbed inside the car. As Gregory headed back to the deli, Samantha began cropping and brightening the photos she'd taken at the crime scene.

Just when the detective began to wonder whether he needed to tone down his involvement with her and Jacob's case, he heard Samantha's cell phone ping.

She stared down at the screen for several moments before squealing loudly.

"What's going on over there?" Gregory asked.

"I just got a text message from Ava. She worked her magic and landed me a meeting with a woman named Kenzie Stevenson, who works at Westman's. Kenzie was really good friends with Jacob, and Ava thinks she's got some insight into the shady dealings happening inside the factory."

"Really? That's great. But I'm surprised to hear a current employee is willing to talk to you."

"Well, she's only doing so under one condition. I have to keep her identity anonymous. Kenzie's actually terrified of Collin. And like Ava and me, she's convinced he had something to do with Jacob's murder. We all agree that his enabling father, Chief Wentworth, helped him cover it up, too."

In spite of the chilly breeze blowing through the cracked window, Gregory felt beads of sweat forming along his hairline. He swiped his hand across his forehead and turned down Madison Street.

"Don't worry," Samantha continued as she slipped her cell phone inside her handbag, "I know the chief is your boss. So I don't expect you to agree with me on that."

"My views on this case aren't based on the fact that I report to Chief Wentworth. I know I'm a by-the-book kind of guy, but I do have a mind of my own," he told her before pointing up ahead. "Is that your convertible parked on the right?"

"It is. So, um…listen. Ava has arranged for me to meet with Kenzie tomorrow night after her shift at Westman's. We're getting together at seven. She wants to meet at Barron's Bar and Grill. I'm not sure if you've heard of it, but it's located on the outskirts of town, near Peoria."

Gregory pulled his car over and parked behind Samantha's. "Barron's, Barron's… Oh yeah, I'm familiar with it. Why are you all meeting all the way out there?"

"Because Kenzie doesn't want to risk running into someone from Westman's. There are a good number of people in this town who know that I'm reporting on Jacob's case. So to put it bluntly, she doesn't wanna be seen with me."

"Okay, well, all things considered, I guess I can understand that."

The detective watched as Samantha zipped her handbag and grabbed the door handle. He was surprised at the buzz of disappointment that fizzled in his head, knowing their time together was coming to an end.

"Thank you again for taking me to the crime scene," she said. "I really appreciate it. I'm feeling good about the headway that I'm making in this case."

"You're welcome. Thanks for riding along with me. I look forward to keeping up with your progress. I'll definitely be keeping an eye out for your updated blog post."

"Do you have your new-post notifications turned on?" Samantha asked, pointing over at him playfully.

"I don't," Gregory chuckled, "but I'll be sure to turn them on the first chance I get."

"Good." She opened the door, then suddenly turned to the detective. "Hey, why don't you come out to Barron's tomorrow night and meet with Kenzie and me? I'd love for you to be there to hear what she has to say and get your take on everything from a detective's point of view."

Gregory put the car in Park and stared straight ahead, gripping the steering wheel a little tighter. While he did want to see Samantha again, he didn't want to do so during another investigative outing.

"I'm sorry, Samantha, but I can't. I—I just…"

"I understand," she sighed after his voice trailed off. "You don't want to get pulled into this case any further. But if you change your mind, you know where we'll be. And you have my cell phone number now, too."

"I do," he told her right before a surge of temptation came over him. But the detective resisted the urge to give in to it.

"I guess I'll see you around then," Samantha responded quietly. "Thanks again for this afternoon."

Gregory cringed when Samantha slammed the door. He cracked his knuckles while watching her strut in front of his car and climb inside hers. He longed to jump out and embrace her. Tell her how sorry he was that he couldn't get more involved.

For a brief moment, Gregory considered showing up at Barron's simply to protect Samantha. The meeting with Kenzie could be some sort of setup.

But he quickly pushed that thought out of his mind and forced himself to stay put, knowing he was doing the right thing. His instincts were telling him Kenzie could be trusted. Plus, the last thing he needed was a repeat of what had happened back in Chicago, where he'd made the mistake of getting heavily involved in a case that put both his livelihood and heart on the line. He'd wound up getting burned, *badly*, after the situation ended in disaster.

No good deed goes unpunished, his mother always told him. In that instance she was absolutely right. But not only had Gregory been punished, he was practically destroyed.

That experience was a part of his past he seldom discussed. It was too painful. Maybe one day he'd explain it to Samantha so she would understand why he'd chosen to keep his distance.

Chapter Three

Samantha glanced down at her cell phone. No new text messages or missed calls. She sighed heavily and took another sip of her merlot.

Samantha looked around Barron's Bar and Grill. The place wasn't too packed. A few groups of college students dressed in their sorority and fraternity paraphernalia were scattered around the bar area. Several jocks hovered over a pool table while a cluster of rowdy construction workers stood nearby, guzzling beers and waiting on them to finish their game.

She and Kenzie had been there for over an hour. While Kenzie stepped away to take a phone call, Samantha scanned the notes she'd been taking. She tried not to appear as appalled as she felt when Kenzie shared one wild Westman's story after another.

Samantha practically jumped out of her chair when her phone buzzed. She grabbed it and peered down at the screen. Her chest thumped with disappointment when she saw it was an email from her editor.

"Ugh," she grumbled, opening the message to find out whether her calendar organization article had been approved.

Samantha couldn't deny how disappointed she'd felt

when Detective Harris shut down her offer to meet with Kenzie. She was hoping he'd be an ally in helping get to the bottom of Jacob's murder. But Samantha now realized that she and Ava were in this fight alone.

"Oh well," she whispered before reading her email from Regina.

Hey Sam! Great job on your latest piece. I only have a couple of suggestions that I'd like you to include. Do you think you could break down potential differences between a working mom's schedule versus a stay-at-home mom's? I'm thinking that could affect how their calendars are organized.

Also, please include a paragraph or two on how a family could work together to maintain one large calendar that they can hang in a designated area in the home. Once you send those additions to me, I'll approve the article. Thanks! Reg

"I don't have time for this, Regina," Samantha mumbled before hitting the reply button. She knew she had a lot of nerve giving her editor attitude considering her writing job with *Elevate* helped to maintain her lifestyle. But all Samantha could think about was Jacob's cold case, especially now that she'd received a slew of intriguing new intel from Kenzie.

Sure, Reg, Samantha typed. I'll work on those changes and get them back to you tomorrow. Have a great evening. Samantha.

She sent the message, then glanced outside, wondering what was taking Kenzie so long to come back. Samantha caught a glimpse of her pacing the parking lot, her tight jet-black curls whipping around her face as she appeared to be yelling into the phone. Judging from her crumpled expression and wild hand gestures, it was not a pleasant conversation.

Samantha closed her notebook and slid it inside her handbag. From the looks of things, it appeared as though she and Kenzie were done.

Just as she scooted her chair away from the table and stood up, Samantha noticed a black Chevy with black-tinted windows pulling into Barron's parking lot.

She froze. Her heart suddenly thumped so hard in her chest that she trembled, causing the pearlized buttons on her cream silk blouse to rattle.

It can't be, she thought.

But when Detective Harris stepped out of the car and strutted toward the bar's entrance, Samantha realized that, indeed, it was.

After he swaggered through the door, she raised her hand in the air and waved, immediately catching his attention. The detective nodded his head and flashed a smile that caused a wave of lust to roll through her stomach.

Calm down, girl, Samantha told herself, taking a deep breath and straightening her shoulders. The last thing she wanted was for Detective Harris to know just how thrilled she was to see him. But as he slowly approached her with outstretched arms and an even broader grin, it appeared as though he was just as excited to see her.

"I bet I'm the last person you thought would walk through that door tonight," he said, running his hands along her waistline, then clenching them against the small of her back.

"To say that is an understatement would be putting

it lightly," Samantha murmured. She wrapped her arms around him, inhaling the sandalwood cologne pulsating off his neck. The pair embraced for several seconds before simultaneously pulling away from each other, as if on cue.

"Well, before we get into just how surprised you are to see me, I'm gonna go grab a beer from the bar." He pointed at the empty chair next to Samantha. "Hey, where's Kenzie? She didn't leave already, did she?"

"No, she's still here. She's out in the parking lot on a phone call."

"Okay, cool. What are you drinking?"

"Merlot."

"I'll grab you another one. Be right back."

Gregory took a few steps away from the table without taking his eyes off Samantha. She had to admit, she liked the detective after dark. He was much more relaxed and even flirtier than he'd been yesterday afternoon.

Detective Harris turned around coolly and flagged down the bartender. Samantha observed his smooth demeanor, watching as he pulled off his black leather biker jacket. Well-defined biceps bulged from underneath his fitted white T-shirt. When he leaned into the bar, his flexing deltoids caused palpitations to stutter inside her chest.

"Hey!" she heard Kenzie exclaim.

Samantha practically jumped out of her nude patent pumps when Kenzie bum-rushed the table. She'd been so enthralled with the detective that she hadn't even noticed the other woman walking back into the bar.

"I am *so* sorry about that," Kenzie continued. "My boyfriend is going crazy because I wasn't home when he got off work. I told him over a hundred times that I had a meeting tonight. I guess he forgot. *He is so controlling,*" she muttered, more to herself than Samantha.

"No worries. I really appreciate your coming out to talk with me tonight. If you need to leave, I completely understand."

Kenzie grabbed her backpack and tossed it over her shoulder. "I think I should. I don't want any trouble out of Alex tonight."

"Wait. Before you go, I want you to meet that detective I was telling you about who's new to Gattenburg's police force."

"He actually showed up?" Kenzie asked, her eyes wide with surprise.

"Yep. He did."

Kenzie turned her head to the side and eyed Samantha suspiciously. "Uh-uh, I know that look when I see it. You aren't crushing on this detective, are you?"

Before Samantha could answer the question, Gregory walked back over to the table holding a mug of beer and Samantha's wine. He handed her the glass, then turned to Kenzie.

"Hello," he said, extending his hand. "I'm Detective Gregory Harris. You must be Kenzie."

"I am," she replied quietly, placing her limp hand in his.

Samantha noticed Kenzie's body stiffen, and she suddenly appeared reserved and a bit timid.

Earlier in the evening, Kenzie had mentioned not being too keen on talking to law enforcement, especially someone who reported directly to Chief Wentworth. Samantha had tried to convince her that Detective Harris was cool and on the right side of the law. But Kenzie never seemed to warm up to the idea of talking to him.

"It's nice to meet you, Kenzie. Thanks for coming out tonight and talking to us about Jacob's case. I know that couldn't have been easy, especially considering you two were friends. You have my condolences."

"Thank you," Kenzie mumbled before running her trembling hands down the front of her khakis. "I, uh... I need to get going. I'm sure Samantha will bring you up to speed on everything we talked about."

"I hope I'm not chasing you away," Gregory told her. "I don't bite. I promise."

Kenzie let out a forced, uncomfortable laugh. "I'm sure you don't. I just have to get home." She turned to Samantha. "Thanks again for meeting with me. I hope that info I shared with you will help bring justice to Jacob."

Samantha reached out and gave her a hug. "I hope so, too. Thank you so much. I really appreciate your willingness to confide in me. I'll keep you posted as things progress."

"And I'll stay tuned to your blog. I just love *Someone Knows Something*. I kinda feel like I met with a famous journalist tonight."

"You did," Detective Harris chimed in, throwing Samantha a wink. "I often feel the same way when I'm in her presence."

"Yeah, right," Samantha said, blushing while waving them both off. "You two better stop it before I get all bigheaded and whatnot."

"I doubt that," Kenzie told her. "You're way too humble and down-to-earth for that. But anyway, I'm gonna go. Feel free to call me if you have any questions. And it was nice meeting you, Detective."

"Same here," Gregory said. "Take care."

Before Samantha could say her goodbyes, Kenzie scrambled toward the exit.

"Wow," Detective Harris chuckled, "she really is in a hurry, isn't she? Was it something I said?"

"I think she's just a little spooked by the idea of you working for Collin's father. You know Collin is her boss. Kenzie's terrified of what may happen to her if word gets out that she's been talking to us."

"Well, I hope you have time to stay a little longer and fill me in on your conversation with her."

Samantha nodded her head and sat back down, unable to control the tingling feeling buzzing through her legs. She couldn't remember the last time she'd felt such an intense attraction toward a man. Even though she and the detective were technically out on business, tonight certainly felt more like pleasure.

"I do have time," she told him.

"Good," he said, sitting down in the chair across from her. "So let's hear it."

Samantha hesitated. She took a long sip of wine, gazing over at the detective. He parted his lips and curled them around the rim of his mug, then took a leisurely swallow. She shifted in her seat and cleared her throat.

Focus, Sam.

She diverted her eyes down toward her glass, setting it on the table and twirling the stem between her fingertips.

"Before we get into my conversation with Kenzie, let me ask you this. What made you come out tonight?

You seemed pretty adamant about not getting involved in Jacob's case."

Detective Harris took a couple more sips of beer, then peered across the table at Samantha. "I guess you struck a chord while we were out at the crime scene. I saw the passion behind your mission to try and help Ava get justice for her brother."

"Hmm, interesting," Samantha said, trying to concentrate on the detective's words rather than the way his triceps tightened as he clasped his hands together.

"But I have to be honest with you," he continued. "I can't promise that I'm going to delve too deep into your investigation. I am still obligated to the Gattenburg Police Department. My loyalty lies with them. But you asked me to come out and meet Kenzie, and after giving it a second thought, I didn't see the harm in that."

"Understood. Now if I may be honest with *you*, it seems as if there's more to you not wanting to get involved in this than just the Gattenburg PD. You've said you're a by-the-book man, that you respect the chief. I get that you don't want to make waves. But I sense there's something else keeping you from getting in too deep. Am I wrong?"

The detective propped his elbows on the table and rested his chin on his folded hands.

"No. You're not wrong," he admitted. "Let's just say that I got burned back when I was working for the Chicago PD. I got a little too wrapped up in a case, and before I knew it, *bam*. I was in way over my head."

Samantha observed how the detective's eyes darted anxiously around the bar. He appeared to be in his head again, reliving whatever it was he'd gone through.

"I'm really sorry to hear that, Detective. But obviously you came out of it unscathed, right?"

"Barely," he mumbled, finally making eye contact with her. "I'm telling you, that time in my life was crazy. It all went down right before I moved to Gattenburg. Actually, that experience was the primary reason why I moved the Gattenburg."

"Really? It was so bad that you had to leave town?"

Detective Harris drained his mug of beer, then swiped a napkin roughly across his mouth. "Yep. It was. But enough of all that. Let's get back to Kenzie. What did you find out?"

The mood between the pair suddenly shifted. Their warm, flirtatious energy had been replaced by an air of cool standoffishness. Samantha couldn't help but wonder whether the situation in Chicago involved a woman.

She was dying to press the detective for more information. But judging from his expression, which was now twisted in frustration, she decided to leave it alone.

"Well, first of all," Samantha began, "I have to tell you that Ava gave me the names of several Westman's Automotive workers she thought I should talk to. I reached out to all of them. Kenzie was the only person who agreed to speak with me. I found that interesting."

"That is interesting. But it could just be that they don't want to get involved in Jacob's case for fear of losing their jobs."

"Or they have something to hide," Samantha rebutted. "But anyway, Kenzie shared with me that she and Jacob worked side by side on the production line, so that's how they'd become such good friends. But check this out. Kenzie is also Collin's ex-girlfriend."

Detective Harris cocked his head to the side. "Is she? Now that puts a different perspective on things."

"Yes, it does."

Gregory sat back in his chair and straightened his hunched shoulders. Samantha could sense that he was coming out of the funk he'd fallen into after talking about Chicago.

"Would you like another beer before we really get into this?" she asked him.

"No, thanks. I'm good for now. Let's keep going. I really wanna hear this."

"Cool," Samantha said, encouraged by his enthusiasm. "So Kenzie and I discussed Westman's second-chance drug rehabilitation program. She told me that most of the employment opportunities go to people with felony drug convictions, especially those who've recently been released from prison. But the thing is, three of the former addicts who were hired went missing shortly after they completed the program."

Detective Harris's mouth fell open. He leaned into the table and squinted his eyes curiously. "Wait, what do you mean, *went missing*?"

"Exactly what I said. These workers just disappeared without a trace. *Months* ago."

"Well, does Kenzie know anything about what came of the investigations into their disappearances?"

"When I asked her that question, she replied with a resounding *nothing*. Apparently, the missing men had been ravaged by drug addiction and all the trouble that comes along with it. So their families and friends had written them off and no one was keeping tabs on them. These men were hoping to turn their lives around through Westman's program. But before they really had the opportunity to do so, they just up and vanished."

Gregory reached into his jacket and pulled out a small notebook and pen. Samantha was pleasantly surprised when he opened it up and began taking notes.

"Old-school, huh," she joked. "Most of us living in the modern world take notes on our cell phone apps. But don't mind me. Do your thing."

"I will," he quipped before quickly turning serious again. "So did Kenzie mention how the other employees at Westman's reacted after the employees went missing?"

"She did. The crazy thing is, they really didn't even have a reaction. According to Kenzie, none of her coworkers gave the disappearances a second thought because of the employees' backgrounds. Everyone just assumed that they'd reverted back to their old ways and didn't want to work anymore."

"Wow. That's pretty sad."

"It is, isn't it? But there is one person who was extremely concerned about the missing men and willing to speak up about it. I'll give you one guess as to who it was."

"Jacob?"

"Bingo."

"Oh boy," Detective Harris sighed as he rigorously wrote in his notebook.

Despite the unfortunate circumstances they were meeting under, Samantha couldn't help but feel an exhilarating thrill at the idea of the detective's involvement in Jacob's case. He may have gotten burned in Chicago, but it certainly appeared as though he was rising from the ashes now that he was in Gattenburg.

"But here's where the story really gets deep," she continued. "Right before Jacob was found dead, he'd decided to talk to Collin about the missing employees. A few of them worked on Jacob's assembly team, and he'd gotten to know them pretty well. So he was happy to see them turning their lives around and getting back on their feet."

"You know, the more I hear about Jacob, the more I realize how decent a guy he was."

"He really was a good man. And what's sad is that Kenzie tried to warn him against confronting Collin. But Jacob did anyway, thinking that Collin would talk his father into opening a serious investigation into the disappearances."

"Clearly that didn't go over too well," Gregory retorted.

"Not at all. The day that Jacob was scheduled to meet with Collin was the last time Kenzie saw him alive."

"Whoa," Detective Harris uttered, tapping his pen against the notebook. "Did Kenzie happen to give you the names of the men who went missing?"

"No, she didn't." Samantha grabbed her cell phone. "I'll shoot her a text message right now and ask if she can send them to me."

"Good. I'd like to run them through the missing-persons databases and see what comes up. I can also casually ask around the station and see if any of the other detectives have looked into their cases."

Once her text message was delivered, Samantha grabbed her glass and held it to her lips, hoping it would hide the look of elation spread across her face. As much as the detective tried to fight it, he just couldn't seem to stop himself from delving deeper into the investigation with her.

Samantha glanced down at her watch. It was already after nine o'clock. She didn't want the night with Detective Harris to end. But she was eager to get home and knock out the edits on her article for *Elevate*, then update her blog with all the explosive new information she'd received.

The detective reached across the table and nudged her hand playfully. "You're already writing out your latest blog post in your head, aren't you?"

"Oh, so you're a psychic now?" Samantha laughed, grabbing her handbag and slipping her phone inside.

"I wouldn't say all that. It's just written all over that determined, impassioned look on your face."

His intense gaze caused her cheeks to burn self-consciously. Samantha drained her wineglass and swallowed hard. "Well, you're actually right, because yes, that's exactly what I was doing."

"I can understand that. I'm not gonna lie, this case has piqued my interest. Especially now that you've told me about those missing employees. Make sure you send me their names as soon as you get them."

Samantha was once again hit with a heady feeling of excitement knowing that Detective Harris was getting more involved in the case.

"I won't forget. Trust me."

"And hey, can you do something for me?"

"Of course. What do you need?" Samantha asked.

"I need you to stop calling me Detective Harris and start calling me Gregory."

She gazed at him. She could feel a shift in their rapport. It was taking on a much more personal tone, and she was savoring every second of it.

"I think I can do that for you, *Gregory*."

"Good. Now, may I walk you out to your car?"

"Yes, you may. Thank you."

The detective stood up and threw on his leather jacket. Samantha diverted her eyes, struggling not to gawk at his athletic physique. When they strolled through the bar and outside to the parking lot, she found herself resisting the urge to slide her hand into his.

Just as they reached her car, Samantha's cell phone buzzed.

"Oh, good!" she exclaimed after checking her text messages. "Kenzie just sent me the names of the missing Westman's employees. I'll forward them to you now."

"Great. I'll look into those as soon as I'm in front of my computer. And once you go public with that information on your blog, I'll have a good reason to be searching for them."

"Thank you again for doing that. And for coming out tonight. I hope you know how much I appreciate it."

"I do. And you're welcome."

The pair stared at one another silently for several seconds before Samantha interrupted the intimate moment.

"I guess I'd better get going."

"Yeah, me too. I'll be in touch soon with whatever info I'm able to find on those missing employees."

"Sounds good, Detecti—I mean, *Gregory*."

"All right then, *Samantha*." He smirked. "Talk to you soon."

He waited as she climbed inside her car and pulled

away. Samantha glanced in the rearview mirror, waving before turning out of the parking lot and speeding off into the night.

Chapter Four

Samantha's eyes shot open. The sound of shattering glass jolted her out of sleep. She blinked her eyes to clear her blurry vision as she stared into the darkness of her bedroom.

But now, as she raised her head and peeled back the comforter, complete silence filled the air.

Maybe I was dreaming, she thought, slowly sinking back into the pillow. She glanced over at the clock. It was almost three in the morning.

"Ugh," she moaned, patting her chest in an effort to ease her pounding heartbeat. She listened. Nothing. It had to be a dream. She took a deep breath and closed her eyes, willing herself to fall back asleep.

Just as she felt herself drifting off, the crackling sound of shattering glass once again invaded her consciousness.

She gasped, sat straight up, gripped her comforter and pulled it farther up her body. Her watery eyes widened with fear. When silence once again filled the air, she reached for her cell phone and crept out of bed.

Her bedroom door was cracked open. She didn't know whether to go out into the living room of her two-story bungalow and see what was going on or hide out and call the police.

Boom!

Samantha screamed as she heard her lamps crash to the floor out in the living room. She ran inside her bathroom and locked the door, her hands trembling as she dialed 9-1-1.

"Nine-one-one, what is your emergency?"

"Yes, my name is Samantha Vincent, and someone's trying to break into my house!" she hissed into the phone.

"What is the address, ma'am?"

"Thirty-five fifty-one East Evergreen Street. Please send someone out as fast as you can."

"I'm alerting the police officers now, ma'am. Are you still inside the house?"

"Yes, I am," Samantha said, crouching down against the back of the door and wrapping her arms around her legs tightly. "I've locked myself in the bathroom."

"Okay, Miss Vincent. Stay in there. I'm going to wait on the line with you until the officers arrive. A squad car is on the way. I'll let you know as soon as they get there so that you can let them in."

"Thank you."

Samantha pressed her ear against the door. There was no sound coming from the other side.

"I don't hear any more noise," she whispered.

"Good. But please, just stay put. While you wait on the authorities to arrive, can you tell me what happened?"

"Yes. I was awakened by the sound of shattering glass. I think my living room windows were busted out. And I don't know whether someone has entered the house, but I'm pretty sure some of my possessions have been destroyed."

Samantha felt her entire body shake with fear. She thought about calling Gregory but didn't want to hang up with the dispatcher.

"Okay, Miss Vincent. I'm making note of that. The police officers just informed me that they're turning down your block now. They'll let me know when they're at the front door. Did you see anyone inside the house?"

"No, I didn't."

"Do you believe that someone entered the house at some point?"

The thought of an intruder breaking into her home caused Samantha to release a chest-rattling sob. "I don't know. I haven't been out of my bedroom."

When the doorbell chime rang out, she jumped away from the door.

"Ma'am, the police officers are outside your home. Do you feel safe leaving the bathroom and going to let them in?"

Samantha grabbed her emerald silk robe that was hanging on the back of the door and slipped it on over her matching floor-length gown.

"I do," she told the operator.

"Okay. I'll let them know you're on the way out."

"Thank you." Samantha unlocked the door and gradually opened it. She peeked out into the darkness.

"Are you still there?" she asked the dispatcher.

"Yes, ma'am. I'm still here. I won't disconnect the call until you're with the police officers."

Samantha found comfort in the operator's presence, despite it being over the phone. "Good. Thanks."

She tiptoed out of the bathroom and slid her feet into

a pair of furry silver slippers, then shuffled toward the bedroom door.

"I'm going out into the living room now."

"Okay, Miss Vincent. Just keep your eyes open and be careful."

"I will."

Samantha squeezed the door handle and pulled it open, then crept down the hall. When she turned on a light and laid eyes on the living room, she almost fell to her knees.

"Oh *no*," she cried, collapsing against the wall.

Her windows had been shattered, and several bricks were strewn across the floor. Just as she'd suspected, her crystal lamps had been destroyed along with her handcrafted indigo art glass vases. The mirrored end tables on either side of her sofa were covered in cracks.

"Miss Vincent, are you still there?"

"Yes. I'm here. I just came out into the living room, and it's been destroyed. The windows are busted out and there's glass everywhere. My lamps and vases are ruined. There're bricks all over on the floor. And now I'm seeing that bottles were thrown through the windows, too."

Samantha dropped her head in her hands. She felt so vulnerable and violated. It didn't take a rocket scientist to figure out who was behind the attack. It had Collin Wentworth's name written all over it.

She had uploaded the latest post about Jacob's murder to her blog earlier that night. Word was getting around town that she was covering the case and looking for leads. She'd been stopped several times in the grocery store, coffee shop and deli by her readers, who would inundate her with questions. They all had various theories—some wild, some realistic. But one thing was for certain. Everyone suspected that Collin had had something to do with Jacob's death and felt that he should have cooperated with the investigation.

Samantha was jolted out of her thoughts when the doorbell rang again.

"Ma'am, the police officers are waiting on you to answer the door," the dispatcher said. "Are you able to let them in?"

"Yes, I am."

Samantha slunk through the living room, struggling to avoid stepping on the shards of glass. But she soon deemed her efforts impossible considering there were fragments everywhere.

"Forget it," she muttered, hoping her slippers' rubber soles could withstand the myriad fragments as she made her way to the front door.

When Samantha opened it, two police officers she didn't recognize were standing on the other side. Judging from the looks on their scowling faces, they weren't happy to be there.

"Operator," she said, "thank you for staying on the line with me. I'm letting the officers in now."

"You're welcome, Miss Vincent. I hope you're able to get everything resolved."

"Thank you. I appreciate it."

She disconnected the call and opened the door wider, her legs trembling as she stepped to the side. "Hello, Officers. Please, come in."

A short, stubby policeman with slick dark hair sauntered inside first without bothering to greet her. His long-faced, lanky partner followed him. He was carrying a cup of coffee and greeted Samantha with a nod of the head before tipping his hat.

"Good evening," he said through his thin-lipped mouth. "Or morning, I should say."

"Wow," the stubby officer uttered. "What happened here?"

"I was awakened by the sound of shattering glass. So I hid in the bathroom and called nine-one-one. When you all arrived, I came out to the living room and saw all this damage that was done."

"Yeah, this is pretty messed up," the officer said nonchalantly. He walked over to the couch and bent down, taking a closer look at the broken lamps.

The sound of glass crunching underneath his shoes, along with his lackluster demeanor, sent a streak of anger through Samantha.

"So, I'm sorry, what's your name?" she asked the stubby one.

"Officer Baxter. That's Officer Miller," he mumbled.

Samantha opened the notes app on her phone and typed in both of their names. "Okay, Officer Baxter, you're asking me what happened, but neither you nor Officer Miller are recording my statement."

"I am so sorry, Miss Vincent," Officer Miller said, quickly whipping a notepad out of his back pocket. "I'm just shocked by all this damage. Can you tell us what happened here?"

Samantha watched as he walked around the room eyeing the wreckage while Officer Baxter stood in one spot, glaring at his partner angrily. She resisted the urge to shake her head and instead focused on Officer Miller.

"I heard the sound of broken glass," she began, "hid inside the bathroom and called nine-one-one. When you all arrived, I came out here and saw all this damage that had been done."

"Any idea why someone would vandalize your property to this extent?" Officer Miller asked.

"Well, I run a true crime cold case blog called *Someone Knows Something*, and I'm currently covering Jacob Jennings's murder investigation—"

"Murder." Officer Baxter snorted. "Jacob wasn't murdered. Everybody knows he overdosed on—"

"Come on, Baxter," Officer Miller interrupted before turning back to Samantha. "I'm sorry, Miss Vincent. Please, continue."

"Thank you," she murmured, tightening the belt on her robe and folding her arms in front of her. "I was saying that I'm covering Jacob Jennings's murder investigation on my blog. And I find it awfully coincidental that this happened after I posted a pretty controversial update today where I called out the general manager of Westman's Automotive Factory, Collin Wentworth. I'm sure you two have heard of him."

"Of course we've heard of Collin," Officer Baxter barked. "He's Chief Wentworth's son. Why would you be calling him out in an article about Jacob OD'ing on drugs?"

As he waited for Samantha to respond, the policeman poked out his chest and gripped his holster. His hostile behavior told her everything she needed to know about his thoughts on Collin's involvement in Jacob's death.

While Samantha wanted to open up to Officer Miller, she questioned just how much she should share in the presence of Officer Baxter. It was becoming clearer by the second that he was not on her side.

"I just wondered whether the blog post hit a nerve,"

she continued carefully, "and someone did this as a warning. Maybe to try and convince me to stop reporting on the case."

Officer Baxter bent down and picked up one of the bricks off the floor. Samantha was surprised to see that he'd done so without wearing a glove. Now his fingerprints would be on it as well as the perpetrator's. She glanced over at Officer Miller, hoping he'd reprimand Officer Baxter for tainting the crime scene. But he was so busy staring down at his notepad that he hadn't even noticed.

"Welp, first of all," Officer Baxter began, "I think I'd be pissed off, too, if I was being accused of something I didn't do on some random blog. So, Samantha, is it?"

"Yes," she snapped.

"You have to be careful going around blaming folks for crimes they didn't commit," he continued. "The medical examiner ruled that Jacob's cause of death was an accidental drug overdose."

"You mean the same medical examiner who has a very close relationship with Chief Wentworth as well as every important official in Gattenburg?"

"Look, I'm not going there with you. Now I know word around town is that Jacob *may* have been murdered. But you're not gonna help solve anything by inserting your uneducated, uninformed opinion. You don't have the authority or the expertise to even be speaking on the matter."

Samantha opened her mouth in an attempt to fire back at him, but Officer Baxter continued his verbal ambush without taking a breath.

"And before you go accusing Collin of being behind this attack on your house, keep in mind anybody could've done it. We gets calls every week about some high school kids vandalizing property all over town."

"Have any arrests been made?" Samantha asked as she glared back at him. A sick feeling seeped into her stomach. It was obvious that he was team Collin all the way.

"Unfortunately, no." Officer Baxter sighed nonchalantly. "But we're workin' on it." He tossed the brick he'd been holding down onto the couch and turned to Officer Miller. "You got everything you need?"

Samantha looked over at Officer Miller, confident that he would step up and be of more assistance than his defiant partner. But when he avoided her gaze and nodded his head at his partner, her expectations quickly faded.

"Yeah, I think I've got enough," Officer Miller replied, closing his notepad and sliding it inside his back pocket. "Miss Vincent, I'm really sorry that this happened to you. I'll be sure to—"

"All right, then," Officer Baxter interrupted, practically pushing his partner toward the door. "Let's get outta here."

"So wait, that's it?" Samantha asked, watching in complete shock as the officers stepped out onto the porch. "You're not going to thoroughly process the crime scene, take photos, *nothing*?"

"Like we said, we've got everything we need," Officer Baxter told her. When Officer Miller opened his mouth to speak, Baxter quickly continued. "We'll file the report down at the station and follow up with you if we have any questions."

And with that, the policemen bounced down the stairs and headed to their patrol car.

Samantha slammed the door behind them. Her chest heaved in anger. She eyed the busted windows and fought off tears while storming down into the basement to search for sheets of plywood.

On the way there, she called Detective Harris. At this point she didn't care what time it was. She was disgusted by the way Officer Baxter had treated her and floored after they'd both neglected the crime scene. But more importantly, she couldn't cope with the trauma of what she'd just experienced alone.

"Hello?" the detective said after answering on the first ring. Samantha was surprised to hear that he sounded wide-awake.

"Detective Har—I mean, Gregory?"

"Yeah, hey. How ironic that you'd be calling me at this ungodly hour. I was actually just thinking about you."

"Were you?" Samantha asked, momentarily forgetting all about her home being vandalized. "What were you thinking about?"

"I just finished reading your latest blog post about Jacob. This is great stuff, Sam. I mean, you did go in on Collin pretty hard, but you presented some solid evidence that backs up your claims. And I love the way you concluded the post. 'Come on, people,'" he read. "'Do the right thing. Come forward. Speak up. Be heard. Help bring justice to Jacob Jennings and his family. Because as we all know, someone knows something...' That's really awesome, the way you worded that ending."

"Thanks, Gregory. Unfortunately, the post really struck a nerve with a certain someone here in Gattenburg."

"What, did you receive some negative feedback on it?"

"Worse. My house was just vandalized."

"Wait, *what*?" the detective shouted so loudly that Samantha had to pull the phone away from her ear.

"Somebody just drove by my house and threw bricks and bottles through my living room windows. They're all busted out, my lamps and vases are shattered, there's glass everywhere…it's a mess."

She could hear the detective rummaging around as he breathed heavily into the phone.

"I'm getting dressed now," he huffed. "I'll be there shortly. Did you call the police?"

"I did. They've already been out here, and one of them in particular was absolutely terrible."

"Really? What happened?"

"Well, one of the officers tried to sympathize with me, but the other guy was so abrupt and rude," she insisted, waving her arm in the air. "And they didn't even process the crime scene. When they asked who I thought may have done this, I of course told them Collin. After that? The alpha officer grabbed the beta officer and practically ran out the door. But not before telling me he doesn't think Collin had anything to do with Jacob's death, and that I need to stop with the accusatory blog posts."

"Well, without processing the scene, how would he even know whether it was Collin or not?"

"My point exactly! He tried to convince me that it could've been some high school kids. I honestly think he was saying anything just to take the attention away from Collin. But you already know I'm not going for that. It's no coincidence this happened right after I posted that update on Jacob's murder."

"I think you're right. Did you happen to get the police officers' names?"

"I sure did."

"Good. I'll see to it that the situation is dealt with. But in the meantime, I wanna make sure you're okay. I'm so sorry this happened to you, Samantha. I wish you'd called me sooner."

Just hearing those words of support caused her anger level to go down several notches. "I didn't want to wake you."

"Listen. First off, I barely ever sleep. Secondly, I don't care what time of day or night it is. If you need me, call me."

"Thank you, Gregory. I will."

"Do you have the supplies I'll need to board up your windows? Or should I stop by the store and pick up some plywood?"

Marry me, Samantha wanted to blurt out. But instead she checked her basement closet and saw that she had several plywood panels left over from last year's flooring project.

"I do have the supplies here. And Gregory? Thank you so much for this. I really—"

"No need to thank me," he interrupted. "I'm glad to help. You're doing great work for the community of Gattenburg while trying to get justice for your friend. I really admire that. This is the least I can do."

"Well, just know that you're greatly appreciated," she said right before hearing his car door slam. "Are you already on your way here?"

"I am. I should be there in about ten minutes."

Samantha exhaled with relief. "Great. I'll put on a pot of coffee."

"That sounds good. And by the way, make sure you don't disturb the crime scene. You should contact your insurance company first thing in the morning and file a claim, too."

"Oh yeah. Thanks for reminding me of that. And I'll be sure to leave the scene as is."

"See you soon." As Samantha climbed the stairs and headed into the kitchen, she felt the heaviness of the attack lift a bit. Gregory's reassurance had given her a deep sense of protection, even in the midst of clear and present danger.

Chapter Five

Gregory parked his car in front of Samantha's house. He grabbed his brown leather messenger bag, hopped out and ran to the front door. On the way there, he checked the lawn and pathway for footprints and assessed the damage that had been done to her windows.

"Wow," he breathed, shocked by the extent of the destruction.

His chest ached at the sight of huge holes in the windows and shattered, jagged glass surrounding them. It was obvious that the act of violence had been committed by someone with malice in his heart who had something to hide as well as something to lose if he were to be found out.

The attack was a warning shot that rang out loud and clear. And for Gregory, it sent a message that there was more, and probably worse, where this came from.

Just when he reached out to ring the bell, Samantha flung open the door. He'd expected her to have a distressed, just-rolled-out-of-bed look going on. But instead, Samantha was dressed in gray yoga pants and a matching tank. Her hair was pulled up into a messy, sexy bun, and her skin had a freshly washed glow.

"Hey," he said, unable to wipe the slight grin off his

face. He knew a subdued greeting would be more appropriate considering what she'd just been through. But the sight of Samantha made it impossible to appear somber.

"Hi," she replied softly, stepping to the side as he walked through the door. "I know you said no more thank-yous. But I'm my own woman and you can't tell me what to do. So, with that being said, thank you again for coming over. You really have no idea how much this means to me."

"You're welcome. I'm happy to be here and happy to help."

Gregory walked farther into the living room and assessed the damage. "This is unreal," he said, looking around the room in complete awe.

"It really is. But I'm more concerned about my safety than any of this damage that was done."

"Of course. So am I." Gregory walked over toward the couch. "You haven't touched any of the bricks or bottles that were thrown through the windows, have you?"

"*I* haven't. But Officer Baxter picked a brick up off the floor and just cavalierly tossed it onto the couch. Without gloves, might I add."

"Huh? Why would he do that?"

"I have no idea. My guess is that he just wanted to be an ass."

"Yeah, I've observed quite a bit of his frat boy behavior around the station. So hearing that doesn't surprise me." Gregory stepped carefully over the piles of glass that Samantha had swept up and approached the windows. "So who came out with Officer Baxter?"

"Officer Miller. He's the one who recorded my statement. He tried to be decent, but Officer Baxter completely overpowered him."

"Oh yeah. Miller seems to be a pretty decent policeman. But he hasn't been on the force for long, and I think he's easily intimidated by officers with more seniority. And as for Baxter, he's already skating on thin ice for giving out bogus parking tickets around town in order to meet his quota."

"Figures. I just hope Baxter is reprimanded after the way he treated me. And they both need to be dealt with over the mishandling of this crime scene."

Detective Harris reached inside his bag and pulled out a pair of gloves, along with several evidence bags. "Don't even worry yourself with that. I'll be sure to make that happen. In the meantime, I'll process everything here thoroughly, and take these bricks and bottles in for DNA testing."

"You are such a lifesaver. If I weren't so sweaty, I'd come over there and hug you."

Gregory stopped midmotion while bending down to pick up a bottle as the thought of Samantha wrapping her arms around him crossed his mind.

Focus on the crime scene, he told himself, forcing his eyes to divert from her curvy, svelte frame, which was perfectly outlined in her skintight spandex outfit.

"So how do you like your coffee?" Samantha asked.

"Black."

"I figured as much. You're too tough to have it any other way."

"Don't be fooled by my hard demeanor," he joked. "Underneath it all I'm just a soft teddy bear. How do you take your coffee?"

"With a dash of oat milk and a touch of raw sugar."

"Child's play. That's how I drank it back in the day when I was a kid. My mother would indulge me every Saturday morning. But we weren't all bougie and gourmet like you. We used whole milk and white sugar."

Samantha threw her head back and laughed. "*Please.* I am far from bougie. I'm just trying to keep it healthy."

Gregory eyed her figure a little more lustfully than he'd intended. "Yeah, I can see that..."

She quickly turned away and swept a pile of shattered glass into a dustpan.

You're doing too much, the detective thought, wishing he had kept that last comment to himself. He turned away from her and picked a brick up off the floor.

"Once I collect all this evidence, I'll start boarding up the windows," he said in an attempt to deflect from his provocative remark.

He glanced over at Samantha, anxious to hear her response. When she flashed him a soft smile, his head bowed with relief.

"That sounds good," she said. "Thank you. And while you do that, I'll go grab the coffee."

"Can I give you a hand?"

"No, no. I've got it. I'll be right back."

Gregory felt hypnotized by the sight of Samantha's swaying hips as she sauntered into the kitchen. Her open floor plan allowed him to watch as she pulled mugs down from a shelf and placed them on the counter.

"So since those two officers decided that taking photos of all this damage wasn't important," she called out, "I made sure to take plenty of pictures before I started cleaning up."

"Oh good. Smart thinking. I took some, too, but make sure you email yours to me." Gregory picked up the rest of the bricks and placed them in evidence bags. "By the way, I ran those names of the missing Westman's employees through the system. It took some digging because, strangely, none of their names were spelled correctly. But I was able to access their police reports."

"Their names were spelled incorrectly? How convenient. I'm guessing that the reports were completely bogus, too."

"Unfortunately, your guess is correct. The first thing I noticed is that there was no exact date or even time frame listed for when the men went missing. The only date recorded was the day the reports were filed. And ironically, all the reports were filed on the same day."

Samantha carried their coffee back into the living room and handed Gregory a cup. "And we both know those men didn't all disappear on the same day. I bet someone from Westman's filed the report once they realized that the men had just up and vanished without a trace, and no one was doing anything about it."

"I agree. Which is sad. Because it just further proves that those men didn't have any family or friends keeping up with them."

"Yeah, it's definitely sad. But it's also not surprising. Oftentimes there's only so much the supporters can take before they give up on an addict."

"True indeed," Gregory replied quietly as he sipped from his mug.

"I just hate the fact that those missing men's cases were left unresolved. It's as if they were completely forgotten. I've dealt with so many cold cases throughout my career, and it's painful when the families have to live with no answers as to what happened to their loved ones. Maybe that's how you managed to suck me into this investigation of yours," he said before nudging her playfully in an attempt to lighten the mood.

"Hey, if that's what it took, then so be it," she giggled. "Seriously, I'm sure you already thought of this, but Jacob may very well be the person who reported the Westman's workers as missing. That could've been the motive behind his murder."

"I did think of that. And it very well could be." Gregory took another sip of coffee. "Mmm, this is really good."

"Thanks, glad you like it. I buy the grounds at Hannah's Coffee Shop. She actually roasts her own coffee beans. Her secret is that she blends both arabica and robusta beans to give it that nice mix of fruity and nutty flavors."

"Good to know. I'll have to pick some up next time I'm there," the detective said before taking a few more sips. "Listen to you, sounding like a full-blown coffee expert."

Samantha set her mug down on the table and continued sweeping up glass. "I'm far from an expert. I just know the good stuff when I taste it."

She turned and locked eyes with the detective. Just then the intensity of her gaze made him feel as if time had stopped and they were frozen in the moment.

"Anyway," she continued abruptly before turning away from him, "back to those missing-persons cases. The question of who reported them to authorities could possibly be answered by Kenzie, since the calls were placed anonymously."

"I agree. Because my guess is that if it wasn't Jacob,

it was her. Do you feel comfortable reaching out to her and asking?"

"I do. I'm pretty sure I earned her trust after we met up at Barron's. At this point I'm willing to do whatever it takes to help apprehend Jacob's killer."

Gregory dropped the last bottle into an evidence bag, then glanced over at Samantha. He couldn't deny the fact that he was taken by her beauty. But his attraction toward her fiery intellect and passion for justice was growing stronger by the minute.

Reel it in, Harris, he told himself. *You cannot endure a repeat of what went down in Chicago…*

"So was there *any* useful information on the men's disappearances in the police reports?"

"Not really," he replied, placing the evidence bags near the front door. "Just a bunch of filler. And a major focus on their prior drug addiction."

"Of course."

Gregory walked over to the sheets of plywood leaning against the wall and grabbed a board. "Do you have nails and a hammer?"

"I do. They're on the kitchen counter. I'll go grab them."

"Thanks," he said, once again finding himself unable to take his eyes off her as she walked across the room.

"So I, uh…" he began, struggling to find his words, "what I also found interesting is that none of the men's names had been entered into any missing-persons databases. At least not the major ones. And I checked several, including Illinois's clearinghouse and the four federal databases. I even checked NamUs, which you know is the National Missing and Unidentified Persons System. Nothing there, either. That's pretty bad considering their family members or friends could've entered their names in that system themselves."

"It's terrible. On their part as well as Gattenburg PD's."

Samantha strolled over to the window and handed Gregory a nail. When he reached for it, his fingertips brushed up against hers. He jumped back a bit as the feeling of her supple skin sent tremors up his arm.

"You all right?" she asked, eyeing him curiously.

"Yep, I'm good," he lied, knowing full well Samantha had practically knocked him off his feet.

She handed him the hammer, and Gregory made sure to grab the head so not to make contact with her skin again.

He turned around and placed a sheet of plywood over a window. Samantha came behind him, brushing up against his back before reaching out and helping to hold the sheet in place.

Gregory felt a fervent stirring emerge from deep within. His limbs went numb, and he almost dropped the hammer.

"Go ahead and pound the nails in," Samantha said, her lips so close to his ear that he could feel her breath on his lobe. "I've got the board."

He closed his eyes, mentally reprimanding himself for allowing his mind to drift off to taboo places.

"So, um…back to the missing men," he said as he hammered the nail through the plywood. "At this point, since the disappearances occurred months ago, the FBI should've been brought in. But according to the police reports, they were never contacted. So I took it upon myself to enter the names into the NamUs database. I also submitted them to the criminal justice agencies that manage the federal clearinghouses. Hopefully we'll get some leads from that."

"You're so awesome," Samantha gushed. "Thank you for doing that."

"Of course. It's my job."

"You do realize that those names not being submitted is a sign of a cover-up, don't you? Because think about it. Any sort of questionable activity coming out of Westman's is being completely ignored by Gattenburg's law enforcement. That includes this attack on my house. Somebody at Westman's is up to no good. And by somebody, I mean Collin. I believe his shady father and the entire police force have turned a blind eye to his crimes."

Gregory secured the board, then moved on to the next window. "I agree that at least some of the police force is looking out for Collin. And there's obviously something way deeper to those men going missing as well as Jacob's death, which just so happened to occur right after he confronted Collin about the disappearances."

"We've got to get to the bottom of all this. I should check my blog and see if anyone has messaged me with new leads. I bet the comment section is blowing up now that I've name-checked Collin."

"I'm sure it is. The people in this town may be afraid to speak out against Collin publicly, but they're probably willing to say their piece anonymously. From what I've gathered, he certainly isn't loved, but he is definitely feared. And with that being said, you need to be careful, Samantha. I don't want something like this to happen to you again."

Her eyes narrowed defiantly. "If you think I'm about

to let up over this amateur, punk move, you're wrong. This little incident just motivated me to go in even harder."

"*Little* incident? Samantha, I don't think you should diminish what happened here tonight. This was a serious act of violence. What if you had been sitting in your living room when those bricks and bottles came flying through the windows? You could have been seriously injured."

"But I wasn't," she rebutted, her stern tone laced with defensiveness as she backed away from him. "You know Collin did this to try and silence me. Unfortunately for him, that's not about to happen."

Gregory realized he'd hit a nerve. Instead of responding, he grabbed his coffee and took a few gulps.

"Would you like a refill?" Samantha asked, her voice softening a bit.

"No, thanks. One cup was perfect." He emptied his mug then studied the boards. "Looks like these should do the trick until you get someone in here to replace the windows."

"Great. I'll call an installer first thing in the morning."

He looked around the living room and nodded his head. "Looks like you've got everything cleaned up. Don't forgot to email the photos you took to me. I'll add them to mine on the police report and include all the details that were left out."

"So in other words, you'll be filling out the report from scratch. Because my guess is that Officer Baxter is going to force Officer Miller to destroy whatever information he recorded."

"Don't worry. I'll take care of it."

Gregory noticed Samantha's rigid posture slacken at the sound of those words. He felt himself wanting to wrap his arms around her and hold her reassuringly. As soon as that visual popped into his head, he shook it off.

"It's, uh…it's pretty late," he continued, "and I have to be at the station early. So I'd better get going."

"Ooh," Samantha moaned. "That means you're not gonna get any sleep."

"That's okay. I usually don't. Too many thoughts constantly flying through my head for me to ever fully unwind."

"Sounds like you need a vacation."

"What is a vacation?" Gregory asked before the pair broke out into laughter. He grabbed the bags of trash that were filled with broken glass. "I'll take these out. Anything else I can do before I go?"

He watched as Samantha hesitated, biting her ample bottom lip while clasping her hands behind her back. She glanced up at the ceiling, then back down at him.

"No. But I'd like to do something for you," she told him. "As a thank-you for—"

"No, no," Gregory interrupted, adamantly shaking his head. "You do not have to do anything for me. I'm just doing my job, and—"

He stopped speaking when Samantha held her hand in the air. As she sauntered toward him, Gregory felt himself once again becoming both hypnotized and aroused by the sight of her sensual gait.

"That wasn't a question," she murmured. "And it wasn't your job to come over here in the middle of the night to check on me and board up my windows. Not only that, but you collected the evidence that those sorry police officers left behind, then volunteered to update my police report. Don't even get me started on how you've gotten involved in Jacob's case, which you originally had no intention of doing, and—"

"Okay, okay," he interjected, throwing his arms out at his sides. "You got me. I'll let you do something for me. What did you have in mind?"

"I was thinking I could treat you to dinner. Better yet, I'll cook dinner for you. How does that sound?"

Gregory was taken aback by the offer. "That sounds really nice, actually. I haven't had a home-cooked meal in…" He paused, running his hand over his goatee. "I don't even remember the last time I had a home-cooked meal."

"Well, you're going to have one this weekend. Does Saturday night work for you?"

"Yes. It does."

"Good. Any allergies?"

"Nope."

"Excellent," Samantha said while walking him to the door. "I'm already looking forward to it."

"Same here. Hey, are you sure you feel safe staying here tonight?"

"I do. I'm not about to let Collin run me out of my own home."

"You know you're more than welcome to stay at my place if you want."

Samantha paused. Her mouth fell open as she stared into the detective's eyes. "I really appreciate that. But I'll be fine."

He cocked his head to the side and threw her a look of uncertainty. "You sure?"

"I'm positive. Now go home so you can at least get a few hours of rest."

"Okay. If you change your mind, you know how to reach me."

Samantha slowly opened the door. "I do. And for the thousandth time, thank you."

"For the thousandth time, you're welcome."

She leaned in and embraced him tightly, then planted a soft kiss on his cheek. Gregory closed his eyes, reveling in the comfort of her affection.

"Why don't you give me a call when you wake up?" he asked. "Let me know how you're doing."

"I will."

"Be safe."

As Gregory walked out the door, he realized just how hard it was to leave Samantha. And it wasn't just because of his desire to look after her.

"You're slipping, man," he told himself after dumping the garbage in a trash can, then heading to his car.

But as he glanced back at Samantha, who was standing in the doorway watching him leave, he couldn't help but question whether he'd already fallen.

Chapter Six

Samantha walked into Hannah's Coffee Shop and approached the counter.

"Hey, good morning, Sam!" Hannah called out over the loud hissing of the espresso machine. "What can I get for you?"

"Good morning. I'll have a medium caramel mocha, please."

"Coming right up."

Samantha eyed the shelves behind the cash register, which were filled with bags of coffee grounds.

"You know what? I'll also take two bags of your medium-roast house-ground coffee, too."

"You got it."

Samantha smiled as she reached inside her handbag and pulled out her wallet. Detective Harris would be pleasantly surprised to see that she'd picked up a bag of coffee for him when he came to her place for dinner.

After several moments, a beaming Hannah slid her coffee across the counter.

"Here's your caramel mocha, and here're your two packs of medium-roast house grounds."

"Thank you so much. What do I owe you?"

"Nothing."

"What do you mean, *nothing*?"

"Just what I said. Nothing," Hannah reiterated, her wide-set eyes narrowing mischievously as a deep shade of red crept across her chubby cheeks.

Samantha tilted her head to the side curiously. "Hannah, what in the world are you up to?"

"Oh, nothing. Just showing a little appreciation toward my hometown hero."

"*Hometown hero*... Are you actually referring to me?" Samantha asked, pointing at her chest.

"Yes. *You.* I've been keeping up with *Someone Knows Something.* And let's just say I am absolutely loving the work you're doing on Jacob's cold case. Sam, that man was one of my best customers. I knew him better than anyone and cared for him like a son. There's no way he overdosed on drugs. *No* way. He just wasn't that type of person."

"I know, Hannah. That's why I'm doing all that I can to shed some light on his case in hopes that Gattenburg's law enforcement will reopen it. But I'm sure you can imagine how hard that would be. Because, you know..."

Hannah snatched a towel from underneath the counter and began rigorously wiping it down. "Yeah, I do know," she spewed. "But the people of this town aren't stupid. We all know that Collin had something to do with Jacob's death. We just don't know the reasoning behind it. And hey," she said, lowering her voice, "you may not realize this, but practically the entire town is following that blog of yours."

"Really?"

"Yes. Really. Most of us are remaining pretty quiet about it, though, because as you already know, the Wentworth family is pretty powerful around here."

"I do know that." Samantha sighed. "All too well."

"Just keep fighting the good fight, though, sis. You've got our support, even if it doesn't seem obvious."

"I appreciate you saying that, Hannah," Samantha said, reaching across the counter and squeezing her hand. "And thank you for the coffee."

"Don't mention it. Oh, and I hope that new friend of yours is helping you out with your investigation. What's his name? Detective Howard? Hardwick? Henderson?" she asked with a sly wink.

"Harris," Samantha giggled. "And stop trying to be slick. You know exactly who Detective Harris is. He comes in here for coffee almost every day."

"Yeah, and looking for you..."

"What do you mean—" Samantha began just as someone call out her name. She turned toward the door and saw Ava walk in.

"Hey, girl! How are you?"

"Oh, I'm hanging in there," Ava said. "How are you?"

"Same. Hanging in there. Do you have a minute to chat?"

"I do. I don't have to be at work for another twenty minutes," she replied, running her perfectly manicured hand through her spiked pixie haircut.

"Cool. I'll go grab us a table in the back."

"All right. I'll be there as soon as I order my—"

"Large Americano with a dash of almond milk steamed in?" Hannah asked.

"Yes, ma'am," Ava said.

"I'll get that started for you right now. Go ahead and have a seat. I'll bring it over to the table."

"You're the best, Hannah. Thank you."

"Don't mention it."

Samantha led the way as she and Ava walked toward the back of the quaint, rustic coffee shop and took seats at an empty table near the window.

"I'm so glad I ran into you," Ava said. "I've been meaning to call you, but things have been so busy at the advertising firm. Plus my husband threw his back out last week after insisting he could install our new refrigerator by himself."

"Oh no! Why are men so insistent on doing things they know they can't accomplish?"

"Girl, I don't know. But when you find out, please inform me," Ava quipped before she and Samantha broke out into a fit of giggles. "But anyway, on top of all that, the kids are running me ragged with their football practices and dance lessons and tutoring sessions. I can barely keep up!"

"I can only imagine," Samantha muttered, unable to stave off the twinge of jealousy stabbing at her chest. The hope for a family was never too far from her mind. And while she was able to find satisfaction in other areas of her life, nothing could fulfill her desire to have a family of her own.

"But one thing I *have* been doing," Ava continued, "is keeping up with *Someone Knows Something*. And Sam, let me tell you, you are doing an excellent job with Jacob's case. I am so glad I reached out and asked you to cover it. My phone and email inbox have been blowing up with people celebrating the fact that new light is being shed on his murder."

"That's so great to hear. And I'm happy to help. Hannah was just telling me how everyone in town is excited about the possibility of the case being reopened. But of course they're not going to say much about it publicly."

"Of course not."

Samantha took a long sip of her coffee. She glanced out the window at all the happy people strolling down the street, appearing as though they didn't have a care in the world.

"I haven't told you the latest about what's happened to me," she said in a hushed tone.

Samantha was interrupted when Hannah walked over.

"Here you go, hon," she said, placing Ava's coffee in front of her.

"Thanks, Hannah."

As soon as she was out of earshot, Ava focused her attention back on Samantha.

"So what's going on?"

"My house was vandalized last night."

"Are you *serious*?" Ava shrieked before looking around the coffee shop self-consciously. "Sorry," she uttered to a nearby couple who were staring at her through bulging eyes. She turned back to Samantha and leaned into the table. "What happened?"

"Someone busted out my living room windows. I woke up to glass everywhere, broken lamps, shattered vases… It was a complete mess."

"Oh, Sam, I am so sorry."

"You know what this means, don't you? I've struck a nerve in someone. I'm getting closer to the truth, and somebody out there doesn't like it. So they're trying to shut me up. But that's not gonna happen."

"Listen, Sam. I appreciate your passion. But I don't want you to get hurt. We're obviously dealing with a killer here. We see the lengths this criminal will go to in order to get away with his crimes." Ava paused, propping her hand underneath her chin while staring at Samantha through teary eyes. "I miss Jacob," she continued quietly.

"I know, hon. I do, too."

"Remember all those nights the three of us would spend hanging out in our basement, singing and dancing and rapping our hearts out?"

"How could I forget?" Samantha laughed. "When I think back on our high school years, those memories immediately come to mind. We were a mess. We just *knew* we were gonna get signed by somebody's record label."

"Yeah we did. With our talentless selves."

"Hey, speak for yourself! I was definitely the star of the group. But no, seriously, Jacob was the one. He could sing, dance, act… I thought he'd pack up and move to Hollywood one day to try and make it out there."

"I did, too," Ava said. "But instead he got caught up in Gattenburg's mayhem. And look where it got him." She picked up her spoon and slowly stirred her coffee. "Do you think you should back off the investigation? At least for the time being?"

"I'm positive I shouldn't back down. Jacob deserves better than that. I have the platform to help bring his killer to justice, and just like I told Detective Harris, I intend on doing just that."

"Wait, did you just say Detective Harris?" Ava asked, her tone filled with skepticism. "Meaning the law enforcement officer who reports directly to Chief Wentworth?"

"Yes. He's actually been helping me out a lot."

Ava rolled her eyes and dropped her head in her hand. "Sam, why would you pull him into this?"

"Why wouldn't I? If he's willing to help us, then I'm going to take him up on it. Think about it. We have someone on the inside assisting in this investigation. That's huge."

"But how do you know his intentions are good? That man's loyalty is to his brothers in blue, not some woman he barely knows who's incriminating the chief's son!"

Samantha leaned back and tapped her fingernails against the table. "You're wrong, Ava. Detective Harris is one of the good guys. I can admit that he was a bit hesitant to get involved in this case in the beginning. But over time, he's realized that we're on to something here. And he's legitimately trying to help me."

"Oh *really*," Ava snarked, propping her hand underneath her chin. "How so?"

"Well, for starters, he and I went to the crime scene together. He agreed that Jacob probably wasn't high on drugs and didn't collapse into that tiny little space in between the two dumpsters alone. He also came to my house at three in the morning and boarded up the windows after the attack, processed the crime scene and promised to handle the investigation properly since the officers who showed up didn't do so."

"Humph," Ava huffed, her eyes shifting around the coffee shop sheepishly. "That, uh…that was nice of him."

"Yes, it was."

The twosome sat silently for several seconds before Ava spoke up.

"Well, if you think Detective Harris is on our side

and legitimately trying to help with this investigation, then I'm cool with it. And I apologize for what I said about him. I shouldn't have made that assumption. He does sound like a good guy."

"No worries. I understand your concern. But trust me, he's definitely on our side."

"Good. We need all the allies we can get." Ava glanced down at her watch, then grabbed her coffee and briefcase. "And on that note, I need to get to the office. I've got an important meeting with a client this morning, and I wanna make sure my assistant has everything set to go."

"Okay. Thanks for the impromptu chat. I'll keep you posted as things continue to progress."

"Please do. Oh, and by the way, have you heard from Kenzie? I tried reaching out to her earlier this week to ask how things went after you two met, but I never heard back."

Samantha grabbed her cell phone and pulled up the latest text message exchange between her and Kenzie.

"You know, it's funny you mention that," she said. "I texted Kenzie a few days ago asking for more information on the Westman's employees who went missing. Detective Harris and I are trying to figure out who reported their disappearances to law enforcement. We're thinking it was either her or Jacob. But she never responded."

"Hmm, interesting…" Ava shrugged her shoulders and scooted away from the table. "Oh well. Maybe she's caught up with that crazy boyfriend of hers. I'm sure she'll get back to us soon."

"I hope so. Because that information could be vital."

"It sure could. Samantha, thanks again for everything you're doing."

"You're welcome. I'll be in touch."

"Sounds good. Talk to you soon."

After Ava left, Samantha pulled out her laptop. Just as she opened it, she caught a glimpse of an unmarked white van creeping past the coffee shop.

As the van came to a complete stop right in front of the window, the driver, who was wearing a baseball cap and dark aviator sunglasses, revved the engine. Samantha's breath caught in her throat. A chill overcame her.

"What is all that commotion?" Hannah called out from behind the counter, and then headed to the door.

"Hey!" Hannah yelled from the doorway. "Stop revving that engine! You're disturbing my customers!"

As she turned away, the driver reached inside his jacket and pulled out a gun. He pointed it at Samantha, a sinister grin spreading across his skeletal face.

Samantha jumped out of her chair and crouched down behind the table as her stomach fell and she recoiled in horror.

"Get down!" she yelled at Hannah, who stared at her, openmouthed, then turned back to the front door.

The driver laughed and gave Hannah the finger, his gun now gone.

"Up yours! I *will* call the police on you, jerk!" she yelled right before the driver revved the engine once again, then sped off.

"Are you all right?" Hannah asked Samantha, going over to her and helping her up. "Looks like that clown was here to send a message."

"Yes. To me," Samantha said, half to herself.

"Should I call the police?"

"Oh, no. Please don't. I guarantee you they will be of no assistance. I'll reach out to Detective Harris."

"Good. I'm so glad you've got him by your side, looking out for you."

Samantha held her hand over her heaving chest. "Yeah. Me too." She waited several seconds before her trembling legs steadied, and then grabbed her cell phone. Her hands shook with fear as she dialed Gregory's number. When the call went straight to voice mail, she hung up and sent him a text message.

Can you meet me? I'm at Hannah's and just had a terrifying incident with some maniac driving an unmarked white van.

While she waited for him to respond, Samantha gathered her things.

Seconds later, her phone buzzed with a response from Gregory.

I'm so sorry, Sam. I'm in South Beloit for an all-day search and seizure training course. Can you stay put at Hannah's until I'm able to get there? I can send a patrol car out to keep an eye on the shop in the meantime.

"Ugh," Samantha groaned before turning to Hannah. "Gregory's all the way out in South Beloit, and he's going to be there all day. He suggested I stay here until he gets back to town."

"I think that's a good idea. You can hide out in my office and lock the door. Stay as long as you want."

"Are you sure? I don't want to impose."

"Are you kidding me? Of course I'm sure. Your well-being is my number one concern. I'll do whatever I can to help protect you. We've got a fugitive running around town, and we're all depending on *you* to help bring him to justice."

A seething flash of anger burned behind Samantha's eyes. "And I will. That much I can promise you."

"My girl," Hannah shot back. She raised her hand in the air and gave Samantha a high five. "Follow me. I'll show you to my office. I'll also bring you a fresh cup of coffee and a bacon, egg and cheese wrap."

"I don't have much of an appetite after what just happened, but maybe that'll change once I settle down. Thank you."

"No problem."

Samantha walked behind the counter and trailed Hannah as she led her through a door and down a short hallway.

"By the way, Detective Harris mentioned that he'd have a patrol car come out and keep an eye on the shop just in case whoever was driving that van decides to come back."

"Oh, good. Please thank him for me."

She opened a door and showed Samantha inside a small, cluttered office.

"Sorry it's nothing fancy," Hannah continued, pushing stacks of paper toward the corners of the desk. "But the Wi-Fi works, my chair is comfy and no one will ever know you're in here."

"Please. This is more than enough. Plus, you had me at *the Wi-Fi works*."

Samantha gave Hannah a playful wink in an attempt to lighten the mood. She felt guilty dragging her into the mess being caused by her investigation into Jacob's murder.

"Well, if you're okay, I'll leave you to it. Be back soon with that coffee and breakfast wrap. And if you think of anything else you need, just shoot me a text message. Otherwise I'll jet back here and check on you periodically."

"You're the best, Hannah. Thank you."

As soon as she left the office, Samantha locked the door behind her, then settled in behind the desk.

You will not let Collin deter you, she affirmed in her head.

She pulled out her laptop and opened the most recent *Someone Knows Something* blog post, where she'd discussed the missing Westman's employees and act of vandalism on her house. It had over two hundred comments.

"Awesome…"

Right before she opened the comment section, Samantha noticed a new message notification flash across the bottom of the screen. She clicked on it.

QUIT WHILE YOU'RE AHEAD, UNLESS YOU WANNA BE NEXT. CONSIDER THIS YOUR LAST WARNING.

Samantha abruptly pushed away from the desk. Her eyes blurred with tears as she reread the message over and over again.

Think of Jacob, she said to herself as her body began to shake. *Think of Jacob, Ava and rest of the Jennings family. Think of the men who went missing from West-man's. And keep going.*

That was all Samantha needed to remind herself of

why she was doing this. She slid her chair closer to the desk and tapped the New Post button, then proceeded to update her readers on the latest developments involving Jacob's investigation, including the most recent threats made against her.

Chapter Seven

Samantha jumped when she heard a knock at the door.

She'd been tucked away in Hannah's office for hours. After facing the horror of having a gun pointed at her, then receiving the threatening message on her blog, Samantha had been overcome by the need to take action. She'd turned to *Someone Knows Something* for solace and before long had uploaded two new posts and filmed a video answering readers' questions about Jacob's case.

"Coming!" she called out, opening the door slowly and peeking through the crack. Hannah was standing on the other side, her eyebrows furrowed and hands folded tightly in front of her.

"Hey," Hannah said softly, "I just wanted to check on you. Everything going okay back here?"

"As okay as it can be, I guess." Samantha shrugged. "I'm kind of struggling to hold it together emotionally, quite honestly. But the good news is I've gotten so much done. I don't know, Hannah. I may have to start working out of your office every day. How much would you charge me for rent?"

"Girl, please. You don't wanna be stuck back here in this cramped little space. Plus, your home office is gorgeous. I'd never leave it if I were you."

Samantha walked back over to the desk and closed and slid her laptop inside her tote bag. "Thanks, but that would mean missing out on all your good coffee and edibles. Plus, working out of my home office can sometimes get lonely. There's not enough human interaction. I love being here at the shop, socializing with you and the patrons. Except…"

"I know. Except for days like this."

Hannah glanced down at her watch, then looked back up at Samantha wearily. "Listen, hon, it's a little after six, and I've already closed up the shop. I need to get home and start dinner for my husband. For some strange reason, he forgets how to use the stove when it's time to prepare something besides hot dogs and instant macaroni and cheese."

"It is already after six?" Samantha asked, shocked at how quickly time had passed. She slung her bag over her shoulder and followed Hannah out of the office.

"It is. Time flies when you're working on a passion project. Oh, and just to let you know, that patrol car Detective Harris said he would send out never showed up." Hannah pursed her lips and tilted her head, peering at Samantha over the top of her rimless eyeglasses. "Are you thinking what I'm thinking?"

"That Gattenburg's entire police department is covering for Collin at the directive of Chief Daddy Wentworth?"

"You got it," Hannah said before hesitating, then grabbing Samantha's arm. "Hey, why don't you come over to my house for dinner?"

"I couldn't. I've imposed on you enough for one day. Plus, I've got a vast array of delightful frozen dinners in my freezer just waiting to be eaten."

"In no way would your presence be an imposition. Are you sure?"

"I'm positive."

"Okay." Hannah sighed apprehensively as she held open the door.

When Samantha stepped outside, a heavy feeling of dread crept through her body.

Dusk had settled over the block. She glanced down the street warily, imagining that white van zooming toward her out of nowhere.

Pull it together, she told herself, tightening the belt on her coat.

Samantha turned around to say goodbye to Hannah, who was still standing in the doorway. Her tense expression was creased with worry.

"I don't feel comfortable with the idea of you going home alone," Hannah told her. "Not after what happened this morning."

"Come on," Samantha replied, her tone more confident than her feelings. "Don't worry about me. I'll be fine." She grabbed Hannah's hand and pulled her out of the doorway, then took the key and locked the door herself.

"Well, I would probably feel a whole lot better if I knew Detective Harris was around. Have you heard from him lately? I was hoping he'd be back in Gattenburg by now."

"I actually sent him a text about an hour ago, but I haven't heard back just yet—"

Samantha was interrupted by the buzzing of her cell phone. A message notification from Gregory popped up on the screen.

"Seems I just needed to mention him to have him reply. This is him texting now."

"Oh, good," Hannah sighed, pressing her hands against her cheeks. "What'd he say?"

Samantha swiped her security code across the screen and opened the message.

"'Hey, Sam,'" she read aloud, "'sorry for the late response. I just got out of the training. They tacked on an impromptu use of force segment at the very end. I should be back in Gattenburg in about an hour or so. Do you want me to meet you at the coffee shop?'"

"Tell him yes!" Hannah exclaimed. She grabbed the key out of Samantha's hand and unlocked the door. "Let Detective Harris know that he can absolutely meet you here. I'll call my husband and tell him that he needs to find a snack to munch on until I get home—"

"You will do no such thing," Samantha interrupted. "You've been here since five o'clock this morning. I refuse to make you stay any longer."

Hannah opened the door. "Do not concern yourself with me. I'm thinking about you and that van incident. Now come on. Let's go inside and wait until Detective Harris gets here."

"I'm not doing this with you, Hannah. That incident happened hours ago. I will be fine. Now go home and enjoy dinner with your husband. I'll just have Detective Harris meet me at my house."

"Are you *sure*, Samantha?"

"Yes. I'm positive."

Hannah shook her head and relocked the door. As the pair headed toward the curb, Samantha grabbed her hand.

"I appreciate you. Have a good night."

"You, too."

Samantha climbed inside her car and composed a text message to Gregory.

The coffee shop is closed, so I'm heading home. Can you meet me there instead? Thanks again for this...

She sent the message, then started her engine and glanced uneasily in the rearview mirror.

Dusk had quickly turned to darkness. The road was empty, and the block appeared bleak.

She clenched her jaw and waited until Hannah was safely inside her car before pulling off. She didn't feel nearly as self-assured as she had at the coffee shop. Now that she was alone and on her way home, pangs of vulnerability throbbed in the pit of her stomach.

Samantha stopped at a red light. Her eyes shifted cautiously around the intersection. Visions of that van speeding out of nowhere and crashing into her came to mind.

Stop terrifying yourself. You are fine.

But as her knees quivered uncontrollably, Samantha knew that she was far from fine. She gripped the steering wheel and let up on the brake, ready to punch the accelerator as soon as the light turned green. The second it did, she sped through the intersection.

Stay calm. You're good. Just breathe.

Samantha pulled a deep breath in through her nose and blew it out of her mouth. She contemplated calling Gregory or Ava, just to help calm her nerves. But as she got closer to her house, Samantha decided against it. The last thing she wanted was to appear as though she was starting to unravel.

When she turned down her block, Samantha let up on the accelerator and surveyed the street. There were no unfamiliar cars parked along the curb. No strange vehicles were lurking near her house.

"Good," she whispered, sitting up straighter in her seat and squaring her shoulders.

She loosened her vise grip on the steering wheel while maneuvering her car into the driveway.

Just when she finally felt her rigid muscles relax, Samantha noticed a huge dent in the middle of the garage door. Splatters of red spray paint were splayed across the top.

"What the…"

She slammed on the brakes and threw the car into Park before jumping out. Her feet felt like cement blocks as she walked in slow motion toward the garage.

Samantha squinted her eyes, struggling to make out the message that had been scrawled across the stark white door.

STOP WHILE YOU'RE AHEAD BITCH!

"Oh no," she moaned, fighting to steady herself as she stumbled backward.

Fear burned her chest. She peered down the street. No one was in sight.

Bushes rustled against the side of her house. She spun around.

"Hey!" she called out. "Who's there?"

The only response she got was the sound of shoe soles thumping rapidly against the concrete. She froze, listening as the footsteps scurried away from her.

Anger overpowered fear as Samantha darted toward

the pathway leading to her backyard. She flipped on her phone's flashlight and caught a glimpse of a husky figure dressed in all black. He hopped the fence and landed in the alleyway behind her house. She ran after him, willing her boots to carry her faster so that she could get a good look at the perpetrator. She wouldn't let him get away this time.

Samantha sprinted through the backyard and slammed into the gate, opening it. She thrust her body forward, watching as the man ran down the alleyway. He dived inside the back seat of a dark sedan waiting at the end of the passage. Before he could close the door, the car peeled off, its screeching tires leaving a trail of smoke in its wake.

"You mother—"

Samantha turned and raced back toward the front of the house. She jumped inside her car, her trembling hands fumbling while trying to slide the key in the ignition.

"Come on, come on!" she shouted before finally shoving it inside.

She turned the engine on, put the car in Reverse and floored the accelerator. The car flew out of the driveway. Samantha's head almost slammed against the window when she hit the curb. She ignored the jolt and sped down the street.

"Where did you go? Where did you *go?*"

Her fury pushed her forward as she swerved into the alley behind her house. Empty. When she reached the end of it, Samantha slammed on the brakes. Her head swiveled frantically from right to left. Nothing. No cars on the street.

"Dammit!" she yelled, slamming her hands against the steering wheel.

Tears trickled from the corners of her eyes and slid down her cheeks. The seething rage she'd felt after seeing her vandalized garage door suddenly dissolved, replaced by terror.

Samantha looked around the dark, deserted block, realizing just how vulnerable she was in that moment. She nixed the idea of trying to find the vandals and quickly sped off.

Her heart pounded now with fear, not anger. Samantha pressed the talk button on her touch screen and used the voice command to dial Hannah's number. When the call went straight to voice mail, a lump of anxiety formed in her throat.

"Hannah," she choked, "it's Sam. I'm on my way to your house. Someone crashed into my garage door and wrote a hideous message on it. I'll be there soon."

She disconnected the call. "Dial Detective Harris." When his phone went straight to voice mail, too, her chest constricted as if she were in the throes of a full-blown panic attack.

"Gregory, it's Samantha. My home was vandalized again. This time it was the garage. I'm on my way to Hannah's house now. Meet me there instead of my place. I'll text you the address. Please call me as soon as you get this."

Samantha hung up and sped off into the night, anxious to get to safety as soon as possible.

Chapter Eight

"This is not how our home-cooked dinner was supposed to go down," Samantha said to Gregory as she propped her legs up on the tan leather couch in his spacious living room. "I was planning on doing the cooking, and you should have been my guest. Not the other way around."

"Yeah, well, plans change, right?"

Gregory stood at the stove and flipped over two pieces of salmon, then turned around and looked out at Samantha. Moonlight drifted through his bay windows, shining silver beams of light on her. Despite appearing a bit shaken, she still somehow managed to look beautiful.

"Are you sure I can't help with anything?" she asked, glancing around his modern two-bedroom town house.

"I am absolutely positive you can't help with anything." He grabbed a container of romaine lettuce out of the refrigerator and tossed it into a strainer. "But thank you for offering."

Gregory couldn't seem to shake the guilt he'd been harboring ever since Samantha told him about the damage that was done to her garage. He regretted not being there for her, even if the situation was out of his control.

"Hey, by the way," she said, pulling a gray afghan off the back of the couch and wrapping it around her shoulders, "how did you get to Hannah's house so fast? After I texted you her address, it seemed like you were there within twenty minutes or so."

"I may or may not have done a hundred-plus miles per hour after I heard your voice mail message."

"Aww, really? You make me feel so special."

"That's because you are special."

Gregory's heart thumped at the sight of Samantha's bashful smile.

"You're also very tough," he continued. "Considering everything you've been through since you started covering Jacob's case, you're holding up really well."

Samantha climbed off the couch and approached the kitchen counter. "Why, thank you. But I have no other choice. I'm on a mission."

Gregory felt his mouth go dry when she slid onto a stool and crossed her long, slender legs. He turned away and gripped the edge of the sink while running water over the lettuce.

"Would you like a glass of wine?" he asked. "I've got pinot noir and chardonnay."

"A glass of pinot noir would be great."

He poured two glasses and handed one to Samantha. He took a huge gulp of his before clearing his throat.

"So I was thinking, you probably shouldn't stay at your house again until I can get a patrolman out there to keep an eye on it. And you."

"Please," Samantha retorted. "The patrol car you called to watch over Hannah's Coffee Shop today never even bothered to show up."

"Wait, it didn't?"

"Nope. So what would make you think a cop would show up for me? I'm public enemy number one down at the police station."

Gregory walked back over to the stove and stirred the mushroom rice pilaf, then took two plates out of the cabinet. "Actually, you're far from that."

"Oh? And what would make you think that after the way I've been treated?"

"Well, for starters, when I filed complaints against Officers Baxter and Miller over the way they mishandled the vandalism incident at your house, Chief Wentworth promised to personally look into it. He also wrote up both of them."

Samantha sat up so abruptly that she almost fell off the bar stool. "Hold on. Did the mayor of Gattenburg hire a new Chief Wentworth? Because you can't possibly be referring to Collin's father, *Walter* Wentworth."

"As a matter of fact, I am. Chief Walter Wentworth is coming through for you."

"*Wow.* I am speechless."

"And of course we'll be filing another report over the damage that was done to your garage. I'll stop by your place in the morning and take pictures."

"I need to find a stronger way to say thank you. Because at this point those two little words just aren't enough."

Samantha's deep gratitude caused a burning sensation to shoot up the back of his neck. "Those two little words are plenty. Because I know you truly mean it. And you're welcome," he uttered, his low tone barely audible. "Like I always tell you, I'm happy to help in whatever way I can."

Gregory dried and tossed the lettuce into a salad

bowl and added sliced cucumbers, green bell peppers and cherry tomatoes. He drizzled Italian dressing over it, then prepared their plates. "Shall we eat?"

"Yes, we shall." Samantha grabbed their glasses of wine and followed him into the dining room. "Mmm, this looks delicious. The pressure is officially on once I'm able to have you over for dinner."

"Come on, now. This isn't a competition. It's a win for me any time I get to sit down and share a meal with you. You could serve up peanut butter and jelly sandwiches, frozen pizza… Whatever you'd prepare, I would be happy with it."

"Humble *and* modest? Those are two qualities I never thought I'd find in a detective." Samantha laughed.

"Yeah, well, I guess I'm not like all the rest."

The pair fell silent as they began eating. After several moments of sneaking quick glances at each other, Samantha spoke up.

"Everything tastes just as good as it looks."

"Thank you. I owe it all to the teachings of Grandma Harris."

Gregory paused, pushing his rice around the plate with his fork before continuing.

"So, um…not to somber up the mood or anything, but did you get a look at the guy who vandalized your garage?"

"No, unfortunately. I didn't. I just saw that he was on the shorter side. I'd say about five eight or so. And husky. Dressed in all black, in what almost looked like riot gear."

"Short and husky. Well, that certainly doesn't fit Collin's physical description."

Samantha sat back in her chair and dabbed the corners of her mouth with a napkin. "I thought about that. Collin is definitely over six feet tall. And he's pretty slim. So this guy must've been one of his flunkies. The skeletal-looking man who drove past Hannah's and pointed the gun at me didn't look like Collin, either."

"Wait, *what*?" Gregory gasped, dropping his fork so abruptly that it crashed loudly against his plate. "The driver of the van pointed a *gun* at you?"

Samantha slammed her hands down onto the table and gripped the edge. "Yes! I cannot believe I forgot to tell you that. There's just been so much going on, with my garage being vandalized and the threatening message I received on my blog today."

"Hold on," Gregory uttered, holding his head in his hands. "This is too much, Samantha. What did the message say?"

"It said, and I quote, 'Quit while you're ahead, unless you wanna be next. Consider this your last warning.'"

Gregory picked up his glass and took a long sip of wine. "Yeah, I definitely need to get that patrol car out to your house. ASAP."

He hoped Samantha hadn't heard the uneasy strain in his voice. But his concern over the escalating threats and acts of vandalism was growing.

Samantha stabbed her fork into a cherry tomato, then peered across the table. "You know what? I'm tired of being passive and trying to fight Collin from behind my computer. The way I'm being attacked is proof that it's just not enough."

"So what more do you wanna do?"

Gregory watched as Samantha parted her lips and slid the tomato into her mouth.

He shifted in his seat and stared down at his plate,

determined to remain focused on the conversation as opposed to thoughts of kissing her.

When she neglected to answer his question, he looked up and saw a devilish grin spread across her face.

"Uh-oh," the detective muttered. "Nothing good ever comes from a smile that mischievous. Talk to me. What are you thinking?"

Samantha dropped her fork onto her plate and sat up straighter. "I'm hesitant to even tell you, because I know how by-the-book you are. So just keep an open mind and hear me out before saying yes or no."

"Now I'm really leery," he chuckled, rubbing his hands together.

"Don't be leery. Just be...*adventurous*."

Gregory drained his glass then poured himself a re-fill. "All right. I'm ready. Hit me with it."

She took a deep breath, then blurted out, "I think we should break into Collin's house."

Gregory froze midsip. "Wait, I must've misheard you. Run that by me again?"

"I said, I think we should break into Collin's house."

Detective Harris bowed his head and released a laugh so boisterous that his shoulders shook. "Sam, I am a detective with the Gattenburg Police Department. What would ever possess you to think that I'd be willing to break into someone's house?"

"Because you're on my side, and you're working to help me prove that Collin killed Jacob."

"And exactly how would breaking into the man's house prove that?"

"You never know. We may stumble upon a treasure trove of evidence. There could be bloody clothes or shoes tucked away somewhere. Or a laptop filled with clues. Or even a murder weapon."

Gregory covered his mouth in an attempt to conceal his amused expression.

"You'd better stop laughing at me! I'm being serious right now. If Collin and his coconspirators have the guts to attack my home and threaten me, then I have a right to fight back. Obviously law enforcement isn't taking me seriously. So I'm ready to take matters into my own hands."

"Listen, Samantha. This isn't an episode of some television crime show. This is real life. You can't just break into people's houses. Plus, the chances of you finding the type of evidence you're looking for just lying around is slim to none. Keep in mind Jacob died months ago. Even if Collin did have incriminating evidence in his possession at some point, I'm sure he's gotten rid of it by now."

"But you never know. Collin isn't that bright. We might go inside that house and hit the jackpot."

When Gregory remained silent, Samantha threw her arms out at her sides.

"So basically what you're saying is that I'm in this alone."

"That's not at all what I'm saying. We just need to do things the right way. The *legal* way. Now that Chief Wentworth is in the loop, I think we can get to the bottom of this. Because in all honesty, I'm still not fully convinced that he's in cahoots with Collin."

"Yeah, well, I'm fully convinced that he is. And did it occur to you that the chief might be on his best behavior to get you—and me—off the trail of his corruption?"

Gregory ignored her question and took a bite of his

salmon, then wiggled his fork in the air. "Instead of breaking into Collin's house, why don't you reach out to Kenzie again and find out the latest on what's happening around Westman's? I'm sure the employees have been keeping up with your blog. Maybe she's got some new leads."

"I've actually reached out to Kenzie a few times since our initial meeting and haven't heard back from her. Ava hasn't, either."

"Really? Do you think she got scared off after I showed up at Barron's and decided not to discuss the case with you anymore?" He hoped that was the reason, and Kenzie's silence wasn't due to something sinister.

"She could have." Samantha shrugged. "I'll give it one more try before I give up."

"Good. Now promise me you won't give any more thought to that ridiculous idea of breaking into Collin's house."

Samantha twisted her lips and pushed away from the table. "We'll see…"

As she raised her arms over her head in a sensual stretch, Gregory found himself unable to take his eyes off her. From her long, slender neck to the outline of her curves, she completely mesmerized him.

"I am exhausted," she continued. "It has been a long, crazy day."

Gregory stood up and took their plates. "Yes, it has. I was thinking about brewing a pot of that Hannah's coffee you were kind enough to get for me. Would you like a cup?"

"I'd love one. Thank you."

He carried their dishes into the kitchen while Samantha followed him with the empty wine bottle and glasses.

"Now, I don't have oat milk and raw sugar," Gregory told her. "But I do have soy milk and stevia. Will that work for you?"

"Aww, how sweet. You remembered how I like my coffee. Yes, that'll definitely work for me."

Samantha approached him from behind and set their glasses on the counter. As he filled the coffeepot with water, her bosom lightly brushed against his back, causing a series of tremors to creep up his spine. He lost his focus momentarily, catching himself when the carafe began to overflow. He quickly poured out some of the water, filled the reservoir and set the machine to brew.

"So, Detective Harris, when are you going to tell me the real reason why you left Chicago?"

"Whoa," he uttered, completely caught off guard. "Where'd that come from?"

"Well, I've been curious about it ever since you arrived in Gattenburg. But I didn't want to pry. Until now, of course."

"Now that I've taken down my guard, huh," he chuckled.

"Exactly."

Gregory stalled for time by turning away from Samantha and taking two coffee mugs down off the shelf. He hadn't discussed his reasons for leaving the Chicago PD with many people and certainly hadn't expected to do so tonight.

"Where do you keep your detergent?" Samantha asked as she began loading the dishwasher. Her tone was soft, as if she may have known that she'd hit a nerve.

When Gregory pulled the pods from underneath the sink and handed them to her, he noticed a compassionate glint in her eyes. It immediately put him at ease.

"So, Chi-town," he said. "Where do I even begin?"

"How about at the beginning?" she rebutted.

"Cute," he snarked, focusing on the coffeepot as the trickling water brewed.

He was suddenly hit by a jolt of nervous energy. Gregory hoped that Samantha wouldn't think differently of him after finding out why he'd left the CPD behind.

"Would you mind grabbing the soy milk out of the fridge?" he asked in an attempt to stall for time.

"Sure."

He pulled the box of stevia from the cabinet just as the coffeepot pinged. After preparing their drinks, he handed Samantha her cup.

"Why don't we go hang out on the couch?" Gregory suggested. "It'll be more comfortable."

"Sounds good to me," she said, leading the way into the living room.

The detective struggled to stare straight ahead rather than down toward her backside as it swayed in front of him.

The pair took a seat, and Gregory couldn't help but stare as Samantha puckered her lips and blew into her mug.

"Mmm, this is really good," she said after taking a sip. "I can't really even tell the difference between yours and mine."

"So my substitutions are on point?"

"They sure are."

"Good to know."

"Can we be done with all the small talk now? Stop stalling and spill the tea on why you left Chicago."

Gregory stared down at his wringing hands apprehensively. "Before I get into all that, you have to promise me that this conversation will stay between us. Deal?"

"Deal. I would never betray your trust. Please know that."

Hearing those words warmed the detective's heart, making him feel as though they were developing a bond. He slid toward the edge of the couch and turned toward Samantha.

"Just so you know, this situation brings back some pretty painful memories. So bear with me if I seem a little somber."

She covered his hand with hers. "Hey, you don't have to do this. If you don't wanna talk about it, we can change the subject. The last thing I want to do is make you feel uncomfortable, or—"

"No, no," he interrupted, tightening his grip on her hand. "This is good for me. I need to talk about it. Maybe once I do, I'll get rid of the last remnants of pain I can't seem to shake."

"Okay," Samantha whispered.

"So," he began, "I was working on a case involving a married couple who'd recently filed for divorce. Right after they submitted the papers, the wife discovered that her soon-to-be ex-husband had put a hit out on her."

"*What?* That is terrible."

"Yeah, she was devastated. Once we got the husband in custody, I was assigned to keep watch over the wife while we worked to identify the hit man. The husband swore he had no clue as to what was going on. But the recorded phone conversations his wife turned over to us told a different story."

"Wait, so she actually heard her husband making arrangements with someone to have her killed?"

"Yep. She'd had her suspicions, so she secretly installed a spyware smart-card device inside his cell phone. We all heard the man plotting her demise."

"*Wow.* So did you all ever find the hit man?"

"We did. But before I get into that, let me tell you this. During the time that I was protecting the wife, she and I got pretty close. We were spending a lot of time together and developed what I thought was a genuine friendship."

"Uh-oh," Samantha interjected, covering her eyes with her hand. "Please don't tell me you had an affair with this woman."

"No, no…nothing like that. We were just friends. Or so I thought. Long story short, during the investigation, I discovered that the woman's husband was a bookie. He and his business partner had been running an illegal sports betting business for years, and they'd made a killing. The business partner and the wife started having an affair, and they framed the husband. He'd never actually put a hit out on her."

"Okay, so wait," Samantha said, rubbing her temples while falling against the back of the couch. "If the husband didn't arrange to have her murdered, then what about the phone recordings?"

"They were fake. They'd been spliced together and doctored up by a professional who took certain words that the husband actually did say, then edited them together so that they'd blend into a stream of manipulated sentences."

"Oh my word…" Samantha uttered while fanning her face. "That is unbelievable. I mean, it sounds like something straight out of a movie!"

Gregory paused, taking a long sip of coffee in hopes that it would wash down the stinging in the back of his throat. Reliving the experience was more painful than he'd expected.

"So let me get this straight," Samantha said. "The wife was having an affair with the business partner, all while her innocent soon-to-be ex-husband sat in jail, who she led you to believe was trying to have her killed?"

"You got it. She was just using me in hopes that our friendship would cloud my judgment and block me from conducting a proper investigation. Obviously, she didn't know me as well as she thought she did. There's no way I wouldn't have brought in a forensic audio analyst to review those recordings."

Samantha threw the detective a knowing look. "She should've known the minute you two met that you're not the type to let anything slide."

"You would think. I'm just glad that I was able to get the business partner to confess once he found out we'd made that discovery. The wife, however, continued to deny her involvement."

"Of course she did. Man, Gregory! That was quite a salacious story."

Gregory ran his sweaty palms down the front of his jeans. "Believe it or not, you *still* haven't heard the worst of it."

"Come on now. I refuse to believe this story can get any worse."

"Oh, but it can. When I reported my findings to the police chief, he just blew it off and told me to leave the case alone, then took me off it completely."

"Why would he do that?"

"Because he and several members of the Chicago PD were being paid off by the business partner. They'd gambled with him, taken bribes from him…plus, he allegedly had ties to the mob. The chief thought that if we pursued the case any further, we'd cause too much chaos throughout the city. So he swept everything under the rug as if it never happened. That's why you didn't see anything about it in the news."

"I'm starting to think you're making all this up. Because it's just too insane to be true."

"Like they say, the truth is sometimes stranger than fiction." Gregory stood up and stretched his legs. "And in closing, that's why I left Chicago."

Samantha held her hand to her head. "My mind is spinning from all this. So what ended up happening to the husband, wife and business partner?"

"The husband was released from police custody after we deemed the tapes inauthentic. We never shared our findings with him, and he didn't ask any questions. He was just glad to be out. I figured he'd try and get to the bottom of things on his own. The business partner received six months probation, which was a complete joke. And no charges were ever brought against the wife."

"So was the wife able to collect anything in the divorce?"

"What divorce? The wife ended up dumping the

business partner after finding out he'd confessed, then reconciled with her husband."

Samantha jumped up from the couch and once again paced the floor. "Detective Gregory Harris. I refuse to believe that man took his wife back."

"I promise you he did. Not only that, but the husband and business partner are still running their gambling operation together to this day!"

"*Damn.* Well, I certainly can't blame you for leaving Chicago behind." Samantha gazed up at him, her eyes softening sympathetically. "Now I understand why you were so hesitant to get involved in Jacob's case with me. But I can assure you that my intentions are pure, and—"

"Samantha, please," he interrupted. "You don't even have to go there with me. I know you just want justice for Jacob and his family. And while it did take me a minute to come around after everything I've been through, once I realized who you are, I knew I had to help you."

She reached over and gently placed her hand on his shoulder. "I'm glad you're here in Gattenburg now. This town needs you. *I* need you."

"Thank you," he whispered.

Gregory took a step closer to her. The pair studied one another, as if waiting to see what the other would do next.

Just as the detective leaned in toward her, Samantha dropped her head and turned to the couch.

"I'm exhausted," she said, grabbing the throw blanket and folding it neatly. "I'd better get to bed. I really appreciate you letting me stay here tonight."

Gregory felt a thud of disappointment drop in his chest. "Of course. I've already got everything set up in the guest bedroom and bathroom for you. If you need anything else, just let me know."

"I will. Thanks."

As Samantha sauntered off toward the bedroom, the detective eyed her longingly. He wondered how in the hell he would get through the night, knowing she was sleeping in the room right next to his.

Chapter Nine

Samantha pulled out her cell phone and checked it one more time. She was shocked to see a missed call from Kenzie.

"Dammit!" she shrieked after realizing her ringer had been turned off.

When a car horn blasted behind her, Samantha jumped and looked up at the light that had just turned green. She glanced in her rearview mirror. An old man was pointing his finger at her, his wrinkled face snarled in disdain. She waved at him apologetically and hit the accelerator, then pulled over and quickly dialed Kenzie back.

"Hello?" Kenzie breathed into the phone.

"Hey! It's Samantha. I'm so sorry I missed your call. Ava and I have been worried sick about you. Why'd you disappear on us?"

"I—I'm not going to be able to discuss Jacob's case with you anymore."

Samantha felt a twinge of disappointment tighten inside her chest. "Really? Why not? What's going on?"

"Listen, I can't talk for long," Kenzie whispered nervously. "Alex is in the other room. But I'm hearing rumors that Collin is in the drug business and Jacob was somehow tangled up in it."

Samantha closed her eyes and leaned her head back against the seat. "Oh no," she moaned. "What makes you say that?"

"I don't have any solid proof, but that's been the buzz around Westman's. And with Jacob turning up dead and those other guys going missing, this is all getting too dangerous for me, Sam. I really wanna help you and Ava, but… I'm sorry. This is gonna have to be our last conversation."

"But wait, can't you just—"

Before Samantha could finish, Kenzie disconnected the call.

Samantha pulled the phone away from her ear and stared at it in disbelief. A streak of fiery anger shot through her. She tore away from the curb and sped down the street.

"What in the hell are you doing?" she asked herself. But as she turned down Everhart Avenue and eyed Westman's Automotive Factory, Samantha knew exactly what she was *planning* to do. Now it was just a matter of whether or not she would actually go through with it.

Gregory is gonna be livid, she thought while slowly creeping down the street.

She stopped the car right before she reached the factory's parking lot and scanned the rows of vehicles. There, in front of the Reserved for General Manager sign, was Collin's obnoxious silver pickup truck. Its enormous wheels and bright red flames lining the doors could be spotted from a mile away.

"So he's here," Samantha muttered. "Good."

She hit the accelerator and sped down the street.

Guilt stabbed the pit of her stomach as she thought back on the conversation she'd had with Gregory that morning.

Right before he left for work, the detective made her promise that she would go straight to Hannah's Coffee Shop and hang out there until he could get a patrol car to watch over her house.

Well, at least I'm not going home, Samantha thought to herself.

The fact that she was heading to Collin's house was an even more dangerous idea. But now that Kenzie was no longer willing to assist in the investigation of Jacob's death, Samantha had to find another way to get answers.

Her heart pounded uncontrollably as she made a left turn down Canyon Avenue and drove toward Birchway Hills.

"You don't have to do this," she said aloud. "You do not have to do this…"

But as soon as the words were out of her mouth, Samantha knew she was going to follow through with her plan.

She'd tossed and turned all night at Gregory's house. Between the intimate dinner they'd shared, the details he'd divulged on why he had left Chicago and the fiery attraction she felt toward him, Samantha had barely gotten any sleep. But in spite of all that, she was now wide-awake and completely wired.

Since she'd begun covering Jacob's case, Samantha had tried to play by the rules. She'd hoped that her investigative blog posts would generate clues rather than the threats she had been getting. But at this point she'd had it. Being run out of her own home was the last straw. She refused to sit back and wait for Collin to execute another attack. Samantha was ready to take action and start fighting fire with fire.

She made a right turn down Sixteenth Street. An intense wave of heat stung her skin when Collin's block appeared up ahead.

Samantha rolled down the window and inhaled deeply, allowing the chilly air to calm her frazzled nerves. Despite the words of doubt flying through her head, she knew that she'd come too far to turn back now.

She made a sharp left onto Birchway Avenue and let up on the accelerator. Her breathing quickened when Collin's three-story brick townhome came into view.

Samantha suddenly felt herself beginning to panic. Her muscles tensed up as she pressed down on the brake. She swiveled her head from side to side, searching the street for neighbors or passersby.

No one was around.

Stay calm. You can do this...

But in that moment, Samantha couldn't do it. She floored the gas pedal and sped down the street, flying past Collin's house and exiting Birchway Hills.

As she slammed on her brakes at a stop sign, the memory of her shattered living room windows flashed through her mind. Thoughts of bricks and glass bottles lying in the midst of her broken lamps and vases came rushing back.

Samantha thought about the threatening messages left on her blog, the man in the van pointing a gun at her and the devastating sight of her damaged garage door. That, along with Jacob's unsolved murder, his family's grief and the missing Westman's workers, was all it took for her to make an abrupt U-turn.

"Sorry, Gregory, but I have to do this," she muttered aloud, speeding down the street toward Collin's town house.

Samantha parked her car a few houses away from his. She slowly stepped out of the car and tried to walk as casually as she could despite her trembling calves.

She cautiously approached his home, eyeing the cherrywood front door and surrounding windows while wondering exactly how she was going to make her way inside.

Guess I didn't think this all the way through...

The likelihood of there being an open window was slim to none considering it was almost wintertime. Samantha highly doubted she'd be lucky enough for the door to be unlocked. And she hadn't even considered the fact that Collin might have an alarm system installed.

Girl, what are you doing?

"This," Samantha grunted under her breath as she approached the side of Collin's house. "This is what I'm doing."

Her eyes darted along his perfectly manicured lawn and miniature evergreens. She scanned the doorway and windows for security cameras. There were none.

Samantha tiptoed down the concrete driveway toward the backyard. It was guarded by a tall wooden fence. She pressed the lever on the black iron handle and gently opened the gate.

She was surprised to see lush green bergenia plants and vibrant red twig dogwood shrubs planted among more evergreens. Samantha didn't take Collin to be the nurturing gardener type, considering his ruthless nature. But looking around at the birdhouse he'd hung from a lacebark elm tree and leafy greens he'd planted near the back fence, she was clearly mistaken.

She pulled her black leather gloves out of her pocket and slipped them on. After glancing over in the neighbors' backyards to make sure no one was looking, she approached the large double-hung windows along the back of the house.

Samantha gripped the bottoms of the frames, struggling to pull them up on the off chance that one of them might be unlocked.

"Dammit," she mumbled after none of them budged.

She set out toward the other side of the house. On the way there, Samantha passed a pair of glass French doors. The blinds were open. She shielded her eyes with her hands and peered inside.

Her mouth fell open at the sight of Collin's sparkling, modern white kitchen, elegant glass dining room table and white leather chairs. The interior of his home appeared to be just as flawless as the exterior.

Samantha was convinced that either Collin's mother or some other woman had decorated the house. There was no way a man that wild could maintain such tasteful order.

"But he is a sociopath, so there's that…" she reminded herself as an image of Christian Bale's character in *American Psycho* came to mind.

Samantha paused. She thought about Gregory. He'd been so against her doing this, and for good reason. She threw her hands in her air, wondering what the hell she was doing.

When Samantha dropped her arms down by her sides, her coat's wrist strap looped around the door handle. Just as she pulled her arm away in an attempt to free her sleeve, the handle twisted, and the door popped open.

She froze. Her jaw tightened as she turned and quickly looked around her.

This is a sign, she thought, stumbling backward when a gust of wind blew the door farther open.

There's something here I'm meant to find...

Samantha shuffled her feet, contemplating her next move. There was still no one in sight.

You have more to gain than you have to lose, she thought before slipping inside the house and closing the door behind her.

"Okay, where to start," she said, her eyes darting around the room. She rubbed her hands together vigorously, then loosened the belt on her coat after growing warm with anxiety.

Just get in and get out...

Samantha stepped carefully across the birch hardwood floors. The dining room area opened into the family room, where a beige suede sectional surrounded a wrought iron coffee table. She peered around, noticing that everything was completely spotless. There wasn't a plate, a glass, a piece of clothing lying around...nothing. The house appeared to be more of a model than lived-in home.

She headed over to the stairs and climbed them two at a time. A couple of bedrooms were located on the top floor. The first one looked to be for guests, considering the neutral-colored bedding appeared untouched and there were no personal effects or photos in the room.

Samantha checked the dresser drawers. They were empty. She looked underneath the bed. Nothing there. She glanced inside the closet. There were a couple of winter coats and sweaters hanging up. The shelves were completely bare.

"Please don't tell me I went through all this for nothing," Samantha muttered.

She spun around and hurried into the other bedroom. It was the master and looked a bit more lived in. Samantha was shocked to see that the bed wasn't made. This was the first sign that Collin may not have been as obsessive-compulsive as she'd thought from viewing the other spaces.

She searched the room, looking for a laptop, drug paraphernalia or anything else that could incriminate Collin. She checked dresser drawers, shuffled through a stack of papers on his nightstand and examined the closet. There was nothing but clothes, bills, shoes and other random accessories.

Just as Samantha got down on her knees to check underneath the bed, her cell phone rang. The startling ringtone almost knocked her onto her back.

She snatched the phone out of her back pocket.

"Telemarketer," she spat. "Of course…"

Samantha shoved the phone back in her pocket and glanced underneath the bed. It was completely bare. There wasn't even a dust bunny rolling across the floor.

"This man must have another house somewhere," Samantha mumbled, "because this can't be it."

She slammed her hand against the floor out of frustration and stood back up. She opened and closed drawers that she'd already searched and rustled through the closet once again, convinced that she must've missed something. This time, she looked inside several shoeboxes, then held her breath while rummaging through a pile of dirty clothes inside the laundry basket. Still nothing.

Samantha slumped out of Collin's bedroom and

headed back downstairs, deciding that the best way out would be the exact same way she'd come in.

As she shuffled through the dining room, a door off in the corner of the family room caught her eye. She initially mentally waved it off, thinking that like the rest of the house, it would turn up nothing.

Leave no stone unturned, she told herself in spite of being filled with doubt.

Samantha gradually opened the door, expecting to see a pantry or broom closet. She was surprised when a set of wooden stairs leading down to a dark basement appeared.

Her eyebrows furrowed with curiosity. She palmed the wall until her hand landed on a light switch and flipped it, then slowly descended the steep stairway.

When she reached the bottom, Samantha laid eyes on what looked to be a high-tech man cave. A pool table sat in the middle of the floor. A gigantic flat-screen television hung from the wall, surrounded by framed sports jerseys. Putting green turf covered one side of the floor, while rocker gaming chairs were propped in the other. An oversize chocolate-brown leather couch sat against the wall behind a wooden trunk that doubled as a coffee table.

Like the rest of the house, the basement was immaculate. There was a bar in the back, and the shelves were packed with liquor. Samantha walked behind it and saw nothing but glasses, a mini refrigerator and a sink.

A laundry room area was hidden around the corner from the bar. Aside from the washer and dryer, it contained only an empty countertop and a couple of shelves that held detergent, bleach and fabric softener.

"You have *got* to be kidding me!" Samantha griped,

frustrated. She dug her fingernails into her palms and walked back into the middle of the basement. "What am I missing? What am I missing…" she rambled.

As soon as the words were out of her mouth, Samantha's eyes landed on the wooden trunk. She studied the brass draw-bolt lock on its front. A keyhole gave her the impression that the trunk was locked. She felt compelled to try and open it anyway.

Samantha bent down, flipped the latch and gave the lid a pull. She almost fell backward when it popped open.

"Oh sh…" she uttered.

She peered inside the trunk. A Chicago Bears blanket sat on top. Samantha pushed it to the side and saw a glass bong, vaporizer and cigar box underneath. She grabbed the box and opened it, digging through several small bags of marijuana, dry herbs, e-liquids and unmarked bottles of prescription pills.

Just as Samantha placed the box back inside the trunk, she noticed a tattered marble notebook sitting at the very bottom. She grabbed it and thumbed through the pages. They were filled with a slew of numbers, percentages, random addresses and what appeared to be a bunch of gibberish, all written in bright blue ink.

"What the—"

She stopped abruptly when she heard the sound of a roaring engine followed by screeching tires. She immediately recognized the thunderous rumble. It was Collin's pickup truck.

Samantha's entire body stiffened as a numbing chill swept over her. She'd known this could happen. Why hadn't she moved faster?

She folded his notebook in half and shoved it inside

her coat pocket, then stumbled away from the trunk and spun around in a circle, struggling to decide whether she should make a run for it or find somewhere to hide.

After a few seconds, she slammed the lid back down on the trunk and darted up the stairs, climbing them two at a time. She could do this. She could get out as he was coming in. Simple. Her right foot got caught underneath one of the steps, and she tumbled forward, cracking her shin on its sharp edge.

Searing pain ripped up her leg. Samantha closed her eyes and tightened her lips, stifling a scream as it crept up her throat.

Get up! her inner voice shouted inside her head. *Keep moving!*

She grabbed the handrail and limped up the last few steps. When she reached the top of the stairwell, Samantha cracked open the door and saw Collin walking through the backyard. That escape route was out. He was waving his arm in the air wildly while talking on his cell phone.

"Oh *no!*" she whimpered.

She thought of the front door. Did she have time? Would it be secured by a special lock needing a key? What if he came in as she was trying to get out?

Samantha quickly closed the door and tiptoed back down into basement. Her thighs quivered so much that her knees buckled, causing her to almost tumble onto the floor. Her injured shin was throbbing. She felt something drip down her leg and looked down, realizing that blood had seeped through her jeans where she'd cracked her shin.

"Dammit!"

Samantha covered her mouth with her hand as tears

of panic streamed down her fingers. She limped over to the laundry room area and hid behind the washing machine.

"Dude, you have *got* to be kidding me!" she heard Collin say. He was in the house now. Good thing she hadn't tried the front door. She'd have run right into him.

She looked up toward the ceiling and saw a vent that led upstairs to the kitchen area.

"I'm already at the crib," he continued. "Dude, I know! I'm so sick of having to hide my weed, man. No, not from my girl. From my maid!"

Samantha held her breath, straining to catch every word Collin was saying.

"You know my aunt doubles as my maid," he continued. "She runs back and tells my parents *everything* she finds in here. Of course I wanna fire her. But how can I? She's my mother's sister!"

Footsteps pounded against the floor right above Samantha's head. Her stomach turned as she crouched down farther against the wall.

Please get out. Please get out. Please get out, she repeated in her head over and over again, wishing her words could telepathically move Collin out of the house.

"Yeah, man. I already picked up the food. I'm just gonna grab the weed, then I'll be back at the factory. And before you even ask, *yes*, I remembered to get your Italian sub sandwich!"

Samantha thought about the marijuana she'd seen in the trunk.

"Nah!" she heard Collin yell. "You know I'm bringing the good stuff. Listen, that's the midgrade weed I keep down in the man cave. It's for the randoms who come through just to hang out and chill. Watch the game and gamble and whatnot. The top-shelf dank is up in the trap spot. Right next to the nine milli."

Samantha's eyes widened with fear at the mention of a gun. But hearing that Collin wasn't coming down to the basement was a relief.

She leaned back against the wall and patted her damp forehead with the sleeve of her coat.

"Please just get the weed and leave so I can get the hell outta here," she mumbled, fanning her face with Collin's notebook.

Samantha felt her pant leg sticking to her skin. Just as she bent down to check and see if it was still bleeding, her cell phone rang.

She jumped up and grabbed the phone out of her back pocket. Her hands shook so violently that it fell from her grip and crashed loudly onto the floor.

"Ahh!" she gasped before biting down on her tongue while fumbling around trying to pick it up and silence the ringer. Why hadn't she done that earlier? Stupid mistake.

"Wait, hold on, dude," she heard Collin say. "I don't know. I just heard some weird noise coming from my basement."

By the time she snatched up the phone and muted the ringer, the call had gone to voice mail.

"Hell yeah, I'm about to go see what's up," Collin exclaimed, "but not without my piece!"

Samantha ducked back down behind the washing machine. She wrapped her arms around her knees and gripped them tightly, cringing at the sound of Collin's feet pounding up the stairs.

Think. Think!

She considered charging up to the dining room and slipping out the door while Collin went upstairs to get his gun. But she knew she probably didn't have enough time. A quick getaway attempt wasn't worth the risk of getting caught.

"I highly doubt that someone would be stupid enough to break into my house, man," she heard Collin holler. "But if somebody *did*? Hell to pay. That's all I gotta say. Hell. To. *Pay!*"

The basement doorknob jiggled, and the creaking door swung open. Samantha winced and recoiled farther into the corner. She could feel the washing machine's cold metal through her jeans, pressing against her throbbing leg.

"Come out, come out, wherever you *aaare*," Collin sang out creepily.

The soles of his shoes thumped slowly down the steps. Samantha's breath caught in her throat when she heard the click of the gun cock.

"You hear that?" Collin barked. "That's the sound of my Glock loading a bullet into the chamber. The next thing you're gonna hear is me pulling the trigger as I unload that bullet into the head of whoever's down here."

Tears streamed down Samantha's face. She closed her eyes and held her breath, afraid to make a sound. Collin had already proven that he wasn't afraid to kill. Samantha knew her name was at the top of his hit list. If he found her in his basement, it would be an automatic death sentence.

"Nah, you don't have to hang up," Collin growled into the phone. "This is what I do. I *want* you to hear me blast the fool that was crazy enough to break into my house!"

His tone grew louder with each word. Samantha realized that she was trapped. If she didn't think of something soon, Collin would undoubtedly find her. And kill her.

As she frantically scanned the laundry room in search of some sort of weapon, the doorbell rang.

"Man, what the f—" Collin griped. His shoes screeched against the floor as the doorbell rang several times. "I'm coming!" he yelled while running back up the stairs. "Uh-uh, it's all good. Whoever's in this basement ain't gettin' out!"

When Samantha heard Collin stomping across the floor above her head, she silently thanked the universe for the gift of more time.

"Oh!" he bellowed, his voice traveling through the vent. "My extra TV screens and poker table are here."

Samantha listened as the front door opened. She once again thought about making a run for it and escaping out the back door. But she didn't think she'd make it without being seen.

"Yep, bring it all in," Collin said. "But just leave it in the living room for now. I'm dealing with a pest control problem in the basement. I'll have my boys help me take this stuff down later."

Samantha hopped up so quickly that she almost tumbled over. Crouching down in the corner had caused her legs to fall asleep. But she couldn't focus on the numbness or the gash in her shin. She had to figure out a way to escape Collin's house.

She held her hands to her face and paced the laundry area.

When she reached the far end of room, Samantha noticed a white folding door that blended into the wall.

She slowly opened it. A dark, partially renovated alcove was on the other side.

A bolt of hope shot through Samantha's chest. She slipped inside the nook and pulled the folding door shut, then climbed up on the wooden bench that sat below a frosted arched window.

She carefully pressed her hands against the window, which upon further inspection, appeared to be fixed and unable to open.

"Dammit!" she hissed.

Please don't do this to me, Samantha thought while gripping the handles along each pane. *Please open. Please open...*

"Yep, thanks, guys," Collin called out. "I appreciate you!"

The next thing she heard was the sound of the front door slamming.

She yanked the handles as hard as she could. The window didn't budge.

"Naw, man, I'm telling you, you need to stay on the phone and hear this!" Collin laughed. "I'm about to go back down into the basement and exterminate the rodent that invaded my space!"

Just as Collin bounced down the stairs, Samantha gave the window one last yank. She almost fell backward when it flew open.

A silent sob of relief shook her entire body. Samantha clutched the windowpane and scaled the wall with her toes. She struggled to pull her body up. When the gash in her calf scraped the wall, a burning pain shot up her leg. She clenched her teeth, determined to ignore the agony and escape the basement.

"Get out here, you coward!" Collin yelled. "My nine and I got something we'd like to discuss with you!"

That was all Samantha needed to hear to pull herself out of the window. She tumbled onto the side of the house and hopped up, then hobbled toward the front yard.

The delivery truck was pulling away from the curb. She bit her bottom lip and limped into the street, shuffling alongside the truck in an attempt to stay hidden from Collin's house.

Her breathing quickened as she rummaged around inside her pocket for her car key. When the remote fell into her palm, she yanked it out, frantically pressing the fob.

Samantha tumbled onto her car and snatched open the door. She quickly climbed inside, picking up her injured leg and groaning while dragging it over the door sill. She fumbled with the key for several seconds before it finally slid inside the ignition.

"Let's go, let's go, let's go," she cried out, turning the engine, then slamming the door shut. Her right foot got caught underneath the brake pedal as she rushed to get the hell out of there.

"Come on!" Samantha screamed. She wiggled in her seat until finally freeing her foot, then stomped on the brake and threw the gearshift into Drive.

Her chest filled with thick waves of panic. She peeled away from the curb and tore down the street as thin streams of air poured from her mouth.

"Calm down," she choked, pressing her hand against her neck and massaging it rigorously.

Just before she turned the corner, Samantha glanced in the rearview mirror. She watched as Collin came rushing out of his house, his head swiveling from side to side as he searched the block. He was still holding his gun in his hand.

"This was too much," she sobbed. "This was *way* too close."

Her entire body shook uncontrollably when she realized just how close she'd come to getting herself killed.

Samantha grabbed her cell phone and called Gregory. The call went straight to voice mail, and it took everything in her not to completely break down.

"Gregory," she choked, "it's Sam. I spoke to Kenzie earlier today, and she told me that she thinks Collin is in the drug business. So I…" She paused, unable to admit that she'd broken into Collin's house. "I just *really* need to talk to you. No, actually, I really need to see you. Please call me as soon as you get this."

She disconnected the call and sped down the street, anxious to lock herself inside her house and wait on Detective Harris to get there.

Chapter Ten

"Seriously, Samantha," Gregory stressed as he paced her living room floor. "What in the hell would possess you to break into Collin's house? I thought you were kidding when you made that, that *outrageous* suggestion over dinner. What were you thinking?"

"For the tenth time, the door opened accidentally. I stepped through it. Maybe someone was in jeopardy," she said, clearly pretending. "Besides, I was triggered by the phone call with Kenzie. Plus Collin violated my home first, remember? On more than one occasion, might I add. Now, I can agree that what I did today was dangerous. But Collin deserved it."

Gregory turned and faced her, his eyebrows shooting up so high that they practically touched his hairline. "Wait, you actually think there's a difference between breaking into someone's house and what you did today?"

"Yes," Samantha snipped, defiantly folding her arms in front of her and plopping down onto the couch. "There is."

The detective could see the lingering fear behind her rebellious glare. He knew she was fighting to conceal how shaken up the run-in at Collin's house had left her.

"Well, let me ask you this," he said. "Did Collin invite you over?"

"No."

"Was he home when you got there?"

"No."

"Did you have permission to enter his house? Or did you just stroll through the door without—"

"Yes, I did just stroll through the door. The open door. As I said, someone could have been hurt and—"

"And you should have just called for help, not gone in," he said.

"Okay, okay," Samantha interrupted. "I get it. I shouldn't have gone inside Collin's home. But I did. And as a result, I got my hands on some explosive information," she insisted, grabbing the notebook she'd found in his trunk. "Accidentally. I found it accidentally and meant to put it back, but things happened," she said, hardly making an effort to cover her guilt.

When Gregory threw her a doubtful side eye, Samantha patted the seat next to her.

"Please," she continued, "come on. Sit down so we can put a plan together on what we're going to do with all this new intel that I—"

"Excuse me," Gregory interjected. "But what exactly am I supposed to do with the *new intel* you stole out of Collin's house? Go to Chief Wentworth and tell him that his son is selling drugs, and the reason why I know is because Samantha Vincent entered his home illegally and lifted his drug ledger? I just—I can't..."

Samantha watched as Gregory, frustrated, ran his hands down his goatee and stared up at the ceiling.

"Actually, I don't think you're going to be able to go

to Chief Wentworth and talk to him about any of this," she said matter-of-factly.

"Oh, I know I can't. Because, like I said, the route you took to obtain that information is completely unlawful, and—"

"*Gregory.* Please, sit down. You don't even know the half of it. There's way more to Collin's drug operation than you think."

He paused and dropped his head, then finally walked over to the couch and took a seat.

"What in the world have I gotten myself into?" he muttered.

Samantha stopped thumbing through the notebook and turned to him. "Listen, I know what I did was… sketchy. And the last thing I want to do is drag you into a situation that could jeopardize your job. But the men we're dealing with here are dirty. They *need* to be called out and apprehended."

"I understand all that. But—"

"Hold on, Gregory." She reached over and gently placed her hand on his forearm. "Let me finish."

Her touch penetrated through his shirt and caused a sensual rush to shoot straight through his chest. It shut him up immediately.

"Now, as you already know," Samantha continued, "I tried to go the legitimate route and seek justice the right way. However, considering what I'm about to share with you, I can no longer color within the lines. But I can't do this alone. I need to know that you're all in. One hundred percent. Are you down?"

The detective stared at the floor, unable to look her in the eyes for fear of what her gaze might do to his judgment as well as his libido. After several moments of contemplation, he nodded his head.

"Yes. I'm down."

"Whew! Good." Samantha sighed and relaxed her hunched shoulders. "I'm so happy to hear that."

She moved in closer to him and opened Collin's notebook. As their thighs brushed up against each other, Gregory struggled to focus on the contents of the book rather than her electrifying touch.

"So like I was saying," Samantha continued, "this ledger proves that Collin is running a major drug ring. What surprised me is that the ins and outs of the entire operation all appear to be right here in the notebook."

"Wow. That's crazy. In this day and age, you'd think he would've kept this information locked away on a secured computer. I can't understand why Collin would have something like this just lying around his house."

Samantha flipped through the book's pages. "Well, sometimes we get lucky."

"You certainly did. So what'd you find in it?" he asked, willing himself to focus on her words rather than the exotic floral scent of perfume pulsating off her neck.

"A lot of what you see here are coded or abbreviated words. But I did a little research online while I was waiting for you to get here, and I think I've cracked the codes on what a lot of them mean."

Gregory studied the bright blue columns filled with random terms, numbers and addresses. "Okay, I already recognize some of this terminology. But I'm interested to hear what you came up with."

Samantha turned to the back of the notebook. "For starters, I think Collin put the most important information on the last pages. See where it says *Chef's Menu*? I think that's code for drug recipes."

"Yeah, I'm familiar with the slang terminology where people refer to drug dealers concocting drugs as chefs cooking in the kitchen."

"Exactly. Then next it says *Diane*, as if that's the name of a person who'll be preparing the meal. But I think that's code for diamorphine, which as you know is the main ingredient in heroin."

"Oh, wow. I agree. Good catch."

Gregory glanced over at Samantha, watching as her supple lips spread into an appreciative smile. He fought off the urge to lean over and kiss her.

"Thank you," she said. "I'm just getting started. You see where it says *meat with a side of fennel*? I actually think Collin's referring to meth and fentanyl."

The detective's eyes widened as he studied the list. "Hmm. Once again, I think you're correct."

"And here where it says *oysters*?"

"Let me guess," Gregory chimed in. "Oxycodone."

Samantha leaned back and threw him a sly smirk. "See, we're on the same page. I told you we make a great team."

"Yes, we do," Gregory murmured, his ardent tone intimating that he meant more than just business.

She eyed him curiously before turning her attention back to the notebook. "And you already know the meaning behind the rest of these ingredients. Flour, cornstarch, powdered milk, sugar…"

"Yes, ma'am. Fillers that would bulk up Collin's product and increase his profit margin."

"You got it." Samantha raised her hand in the air and gave the detective a high five.

"And look," she continued, flipping through several pages. "I think these addresses belong to Collin's clients and possibly some of his drug runners. The dates listed track when the transactions occurred, and I think the numbers represent how much money he puts out and how much he brings in."

"Wow…" Gregory's eyes shifted from the book to Samantha. "You know, while I don't condone how you got ahold of this ledger, I have to admit, I am in awe right now. Your analysis is really impressive. Now we just need to figure out exactly how I should present this information to Chief Wentworth. He's going to be devastated when he finds out Collin's involved in all this."

Samantha closed the notebook and gently placed her hand on Gregory's thigh. "Yeah, about that…"

Without thinking, he covered her hand with his and looked her directly in the eye. "What about it?" he whispered, unable to project his voice properly due to a stirring sensation in his lower abdomen.

Samantha glanced down at his hand then looked back up at him and cleared her throat. "When I was paging through the book, I stumbled upon a list of pickup locations for the drugs. Guess whose name was at the very top of the list?"

"Whose?"

"Chief Wentworth's."

Gregory felt his entire body go numb. He fell against the back of the couch as a pang of nausea hit the pit of his stomach.

"You have got to be kidding me," he moaned. "So he's in on all this, too?"

"According to this ledger, yes."

The detective balled his hands into tight fists. "This

is starting to feel exactly like what I went through in Chicago all over again. The reason why I came to Gattenburg was to get the hell away from all the corruption and foul behavior. And now this." He leaned forward, propping his elbows onto his knees. "I just feel so sick. And betrayed."

Samantha reached out and caressed his back reassuringly. "I'm so sorry, Gregory. I really didn't want to have to tell you that. But at least you know whom you're dealing with now. And you know why I had to act in such an...unorthodox...manner. We're talking major corruption here."

"I do. And I appreciate you telling me."

The pair gazed at one another silently before the buzz of Gregory's cell phone interrupted the moment. He pulled it from his pocket and stared down at the screen, then jumped up from the couch.

"I cannot *believe* this!" he exclaimed.

"What's going on?"

"One of the detectives just texted me. He received word that the bodies of the three missing Westman's workers were found up in Galena in the Tapley Woods."

"Ugh," Samantha moaned, gripping her stomach. "Did he say how they died?"

"Apparently from a drug overdose. Whatever was in their systems was very potent and very lethal."

"That is such devastating news..." Samantha stood up and slowly approached the detective. "Gregory, you know how I've been saying we've got to figure out what's really going on inside Westman's Automotive Factory?"

"I do."

"Well, I think I have. And I believe it's directly linked to those men's deaths."

"Okay. Let's hear it."

Samantha took a deep breath as the pair sat back down on the couch. "I think Westman's is doubling as a drug lab. And Collin's testing his product out on the employees who are addicts. If that's the case, I wonder how long he's been in business and what Jacob knew."

Gregory stared up at the ceiling. "Maybe Jacob found out that Collin was selling drugs and threatened to turn him in. Or what if Jacob was actually in business with Collin and got caught up in a deal gone wrong?"

"I can't see that being the case," Samantha refuted. "Jacob supposedly went to talk to Collin about the Westman's workers after they went missing, remember? If they were in business together, I highly doubt he would've bothered to inquire about their disappearances."

As Samantha spoke, Gregory realized he was more focused on her lips than the words coming through them.

Get your head in the game, man, he told himself. He grabbed the drug ledger and thumbed through the pages in hopes of finding specific instructions on exactly how Collin cooked up his product.

"You know what?" Samantha continued, hopping up from the couch before bending down and grabbing her injured leg. *"Ouch!"*

"Are you okay?" the detective asked. "Do you think we need to add a couple more bandages to your wound?"

"No, I'm fine. I just need to take it easy and avoid making any abrupt moves. But anyway, I was going to say that I think Collin was using those poor Westman's employees as guinea pigs. He was probably testing the drugs out on them in an effort to try and find the perfect combo before selling them on the street."

Gregory nodded his head in agreement. "I could definitely see him doing something like that. And because he isn't that bright, I'm sure his measurements were way off."

"I have *got* to talk to Kenzie. I just need to figure out a way to get her to speak with me again. I have to convince her that I'd never reveal her identity."

"Yeah, that would be great if you could get a conversation going with her again. I have a feeling she knows a hell of a lot more than what she's shared so far. If we could get some concrete evidence from her, I could definitely build a more solid case against Collin and Chief Wentworth and present it to the district attorney."

Samantha pointed at the detective. *"And,"* she began slowly, "maybe Kenzie could somehow find a way to get me inside Westman's after hours so that I can see what's really going on inside that elusive concrete jungle. Because I'm thinking that if he does have some sort of underground drug lab set up in there—"

"Samantha," Gregory interrupted, "you are not, I repeat, *not* going to break into Westman's Automotive Factory under any circumstances. And I mean that. Not only is it against the law, but it's beyond dangerous. Look at what happened to you today when you broke into Collin's house. He could have killed you!"

"But he didn't."

"But he *could* have. And because you unlawfully entered his home, he would've gotten away with murder after pleading self-defense. I don't know what I'd do with myself if something happened to you. So moving forward, let's go about this the right way. The *legal* way. Are we clear on that?"

Gregory braced himself, expecting Samantha to snap back with some sort of snarky comment. He was pleasantly surprised when she looked directly at him with a softened expression.

"Yes," she whispered. "We're clear."

He watched as her eyes searched his face, as if there was something more she wanted to say. He held his breath, waiting for her to speak. But she remained silent.

"Okay, then," Gregory said. "So we're good."

"Yes, we are. I'll give Kenzie a call first thing tomorrow morning. Hopefully she won't ignore me." Samantha stretched her arms over her head, then rubbed the back of her neck. "I am so exhausted…"

Detective Harris opened his mouth to speak. But nothing came out as he watched her cropped sweater rise above her stomach, revealing her smooth, taut midsection. When she threw her head back and ran her perfectly manicured hands through her wavy hair, he stared down at the floor and rubbed his temples rigorously.

"So while you try and get ahold of Kenzie, I'll start digging around in some of the files down at the station," he told her, determined to focus on the mission at hand rather than his feelings of sexual excitement. "See if I can find information on drug busts that have occurred in the past year or so. There might be a statement buried in a report made by a drug dealer or addict that could provide us with some clues. You never know."

"I think that's a great idea. And in the meantime," Samantha said, inching toward the kitchen, "I think we deserve a treat for all that we've been through today."

"Oh yeah?" Gregory couldn't help but chuckle at

the sight of her sweet, mischievous grin. "What did you have in mind?"

"I don't know," she shrugged coyly. "Maybe two cups of Hannah's Heavenly Hazelnut coffee and a couple of her frosted cinnamon rolls. What do you think?"

"I think that sounds delicious."

"Good. Follow me into the kitchen?"

"I'm right behind you."

Gregory stood up and let Samantha lead the way, forcing himself not to eye her curvaceous backside as she sashayed in front of him. "But let me help you."

She spun around and gave him a wink. "Oh all right, if you insist."

"I absolutely insist."

As the detective entered the kitchen and pulled two mugs down off the shelf, he mentally rewound the day's crazy developments. From the moment he'd heard Samantha's frantic voice mail message to finding out she'd broken into Collin's house to learning that Collin and Chief Wentworth were running a drug ring together, it had by far been his wildest day in Gattenburg.

But now, Gregory was just glad that he and Samantha were on the same page and had come to an agreement on how they would proceed with their joint investigation.

Joint investigation.

Those were two words the detective had never thought he'd speak again when it came to partnering with a woman. Yet here he was, finally ready to move past his painful experience in Chicago and take on the investigation of a lifetime with Samantha by his side.

Chapter Eleven

Samantha was so irritated that she could literally feel her skin crawling.

She had called Kenzie several times, leaving voice mails then following up with text messages, making it clear that she really needed to talk to her. But Kenzie still hadn't responded.

Whether Kenzie was avoiding her or not, Samantha was determined to share with her the new developments in the investigation of Jacob's death and see if it would help shake loose any other information. So much so that she'd driven down to Westman's Automotive Factory and was sitting inside her car, waiting for Kenzie to come outside for lunch so that she could make one last-ditch effort to speak with her.

Samantha craned her neck and stared out the window from her discreetly parked car, which sat half a block away from the factory. Her eyes were glued to the back door that led out into the parking lot.

Kenzie usually left the factory sometime between eleven and noon to head over to Victor's Café for the all-you-can-eat lunch buffet. Samantha's plan was to follow Kenzie to the restaurant, delicately approach her before she went inside and ask if they could sit down and talk.

Samantha's stomach turned as she anticipated Kenzie walking out the door at any given moment. She knew she was probably doing too much by showing up at her job unannounced. But Samantha wasn't too proud to admit that she was getting desperate. She and Gregory were getting too close to cracking Jacob's murder case and busting Collin and Chief Westworth to turn back now. Samantha just hoped she could convince Kenzie to spill whatever information she may have been holding, which could ultimately help solve the entire investigation.

She peered in her side-view mirror and noticed a white van coming toward her. Flashbacks of the incident at Hannah's flooded her mind. Samantha's heart began to beat so furiously that she could feel it in her pulsating temples. She quickly slumped down in her seat and turned away from the window, hoping that whoever was driving the vehicle wouldn't notice her.

When the van sped past her, Samantha emitted a deep sigh of relief, not realizing that she'd been holding her breath the whole time. She slowly sat back up and noticed the back door to the factory open. Her cell phone buzzed, but she ignored the call and kept her eyes glued to the exit.

Several men walked out into the parking lot. Samantha peered through the windshield, looking to see if Kenzie would follow them. But the door slammed with no sign of her.

"Ugh," she moaned. "Will you come out already?"

Samantha glanced down at her watch. It was after twelve o'clock. She'd been sitting in that spot for over an hour, and her body was tweaking with impatience.

She jumped at the sound of her cell phone buzzing

again. Samantha pulled it from her handbag and saw a text message notification from Ava displayed on the screen.

They hadn't spoken since running into one another at Hannah's. Samantha wasn't planning on telling her or Kenzie that she'd gone into Collin's house and found the drug ledger. She would just have to figure out some other way to let them know she'd discovered his drug operation.

Samantha swiped the security code into her cell phone and tapped on Ava's message.

"Please have some good news for me..." she said aloud. Her voice trailed off as she began reading the text.

Are you available to meet up? We need to talk ASAP! I just spoke to one of Jacob's old friends at Westman's and found out Kenzie is missing! I'm really worried about her, especially after hearing that those missing workers were found dead...

Samantha inhaled sharply as her eyes stung with unshed tears. "Wait, wait, wait," Samantha uttered, scanning the message over and over again as if she'd misread it. "This isn't happening. This *can't* be happening!"

She tightened her grip on the phone as her hand began to tremble and anxiously dialed Ava's number. The call went straight to voice mail.

Before she could leave a message, the phone vibrated against her ear. Samantha pulled it away and checked the screen. Another text from Ava popped up.

Sorry, can't talk. In a meeting. Can you meet me at Hannah's in 30 minutes?

I can, Samantha replied. I am sick to my stomach right now after hearing that Kenzie is missing. I'm actually sitting outside Westman's. I was hoping to run into her and get more info on the factory. Is it okay if Detective Harris meets with us, too? I want him to hear everything about Kenzie's disappearance.

She sent the message, then looked back up at the parking lot. Collin's huge pickup truck was parked crookedly across two spaces. She glared at it, imagining herself smashing the windows and lights out with a baseball bat.

Just as her phone buzzed again, Collin came strolling out the door. Samantha's eyes narrowed in disgust at the sight of him spinning around arrogantly and high-fiving several of his cronies who'd walked out behind him.

She stifled a sob, watching while he threw his head back and cackled loudly as if he didn't have a care in the world. He and his boys jumped inside his truck, and Collin turned the music up full blast, revved the engine, then sped out of the lot.

The familiar sound of that thunderous roar caused her body to shake in a fit of anger.

"You *animal*!" she yelled while hot tears burned the corners of her eyes.

Samantha checked her phone and saw that Ava had responded to her text, confirming that she was fine with Gregory joining them.

Okay, thanks, she wrote back. I'm heading to the coffee shop now. See you there.

She started the engine and sped down the street, fighting off the urge to catch up to Collin's truck and ram her car into it.

SAMANTHA FELT AS though she were in a daze. She was sitting at a discreet back corner table in between Gregory and Ava, staring straight ahead at nothing in particular.

The coffee shop was fairly packed. Gregory had suggested that they meet elsewhere so not to be seen by law enforcement or one of Westman's workers. But Ava was in between conference calls and needed a quick, convenient place to talk.

Hannah sat the group as far away from the front windows as possible. Once she assured Gregory that her shop was too bougie for the automotive factory workers and too short on doughnuts for the Gattenburg PD, he agreed to stay.

As convincing as Hannah had been, however, Samantha still found herself jumping out of her seat every time the front doorbell jingled and a customer entered the shop.

There was a frigid chill lingering in the air. Samantha was still wearing her hat, coat and scarf but couldn't seem to warm up. Not even the piping-hot mocha latte she'd been sipping on could stave off the cold.

Hannah swore she'd turned the heat up full blast and even started a fire in the wood-burning fireplace. But Samantha knew that it wasn't the coffee shop's temperature that had her blood running cold. It was the news of Kenzie's disappearance chilling her to the bone.

"So this friend of Jacob's you spoke to," Gregory

said to Ava. "Did he mention the last time he'd seen Kenzie?"

She took a deep, wavering breath. Her shifting eyes and downturned mouth were a clear indication that she was terrified.

"He did, actually. It was over a week ago. They work on the same assembly team, so of course her not being at the factory stood out to him."

Gregory slowly nodded his head before taking a sip of his double shot of espresso. "Did he ask anybody around the factory whether they knew anything, or if she was out sick or on vacation?"

"No, unfortunately. Those factory workers aren't stupid. They see what's happening around there. Plus, they're all afraid of Collin. They know what he's capable of. And they also know that Chief Wentworth is going to have his son's back no matter what. So no one wants to risk putting that type of attention on themselves."

Samantha's left eye began to twitch uncontrollably. She felt as if she was about to implode. "We have *got* to do something about this. What's this guy's name you've been talking to?"

"Taylor. Hudson Taylor."

Gregory quickly pulled a notepad and pen from inside his bomber jacket and wrote the name down.

"Did Hudson mention whether or not Kenzie's family has reported her missing?" Samantha continued.

Ava lips twisted in clear frustration. "So here's where the situation gets murky. Hudson is friends with Alex, who you all know is Kenzie's boyfriend. According to Alex, Kenzie sent him an email a little over a week ago claiming that life was getting to be too much for her.

She just wanted to get away from it all. Ditch Gattenburg and start a new life elsewhere."

"Oh *please*," Samantha grunted, rolling her eyes at Ava. "I hope Alex didn't fall for that. Does he actually believe that email was sent to him by Kenzie?"

"He doesn't have reason to think otherwise. Kenzie never shared with him her issues with Collin, or Westman's, or the missing men who turned up dead. All Alex knows is that Collin's her ex. Which in turn means he hates him. So she went out of her way to never bring him up."

Gregory continued writing notes furiously in his pad before looking up at Ava, his forehead crinkling with concern. "Is this the same boyfriend I've heard about who's allegedly very controlling?"

"Unfortunately, yes," Ava responded, "it is."

"Umph," the detective grunted. "Well, I need to start by checking to see if a missing-persons report has been filed on Kenzie's behalf."

"I seriously doubt it," Ava said. "Kenzie is estranged from her family. She's been in and out of trouble over the years. Her volatile relationship with Alex was the final straw. Between his substance abuse issues and erratic behavior, her family refused to stand by and watch her ruin her life again after she'd gotten clean."

"I didn't realize Kenzie was dealing with all those issues," Samantha said. "That is really sad."

"It is," Ava agreed. "And Alex seems to believe that email really came from Kenzie. So as far as he's concerned, no crime has been committed."

Samantha felt a burning wave of anger wash over her. "You know, as crazy as he may be, I seriously doubt that Alex has anything to do with her disappearance.

This is about Collin, Westman's and what she knew. So I hope that law enforcement doesn't try and put this off on him."

Samantha suddenly felt her body beginning to overheat. She tore off her hat and scarf, then glanced over at Gregory, waiting to hear what he had to say. He nodded his head at her and pointed at Ava.

"Do you think there's any way your friend Hudson could get Alex to forward a copy of that email to him?"

"I don't know, but I can certainly ask."

"Good," he told her. "Then if he can send it to you, I can take a look at it and have a computer forensics investigator check it out."

Samantha felt her chest tighten at the thought of Gregory pulling someone from the Gattenburg PD into their investigation.

"Wait," she said to him, "do you think that's a good idea? Especially with the, uh—" She paused, glancing over at Ava. "The *new intel* we just received?"

Ava sat straight up in her chair. "What new intel?" she asked, her head swiveling back and forth from Samantha to Gregory as if she were watching a tennis match.

Samantha hesitated. She glanced over at Gregory. He didn't chime in, but his soft, sympathetic expression silently told her that it was okay to share what they'd uncovered about Collin.

Just don't mention breaking into his house, she reminded herself.

"Ava," she began before looking around the shop then lowering her voice, "what I'm about to share with you must remain strictly between us. Okay?"

"Of course." She patted her hand against her chest

and took a long sip of her caffè macchiato. "Now I'm getting nervous…"

"Collin is running a major drug ring, and we need your help. And we think that has something to do with Jacob's murder as well as the Westman's employees who turned up dead after they OD'd on drugs."

"Actually," Gregory added, "we think that has *everything* to do with Jacob's murder and the factory workers who turned up dead—after OD'ing on lethal drugs we believe they got from Collin, no less."

Ava's mouth fell open, but nothing came out. Tears pooled along the rims of her eyes. Samantha reached over and held her hand.

"That dirty mother…" Ava whispered. "But honestly? I'm really not surprised. What I don't understand is how Collin's drug ring would tie into Jacob's murder, though. He wasn't involved in anything like that."

"Are you sure?" Gregory asked, his low tone filled with skepticism. "Because you never know what he may have been doing behind your—"

"I'm *positive*," Ava interrupted firmly as she glared at him. Her stone-cold expression silenced the detective immediately. Samantha gave Ava's hand a squeeze.

"Hey," she said softly, "Gregory didn't mean to offend you. We just want to make sure no stone is left unturned."

"When it comes to my brother's death," Ava snapped back, "there are no salacious stones to turn. So let's just drop that whole theory. Why don't we talk about finally taking some serious action against Collin instead?"

Samantha gradually removed her hand from Ava's grip and sat back. She watched as her friend began to unravel, abruptly scooting to the edge of her chair and waving her hand wildly in the air.

"Detective Harris," Ava continued, "do you think you have the guts to confront your boss and tell him that his son is out here killing people? I know you're new to the force and all, but we need some new blood to step up and straighten out Chief Wentworth. Because a majority of the men who've been working for him are too weak to do it. He's got them all wrapped around his finger."

Gregory closed his notepad and folded his hands on top of the table. Samantha knew he was hesitant to tell Ava the extent of Chief Wentworth's involvement. So she took it upon herself to do so.

"Why are you looking at me like that?" Ava asked Gregory before turning to Samantha. "What's going on?"

"Ava," Samantha began, "we believe Chief Wentworth is a part of Collin's drug operation."

Ava stared back at her blankly. "Wait, *what*? W-why do you think that?" she stammered, her voice trembling with shock.

"I'm sorry, but I can't divulge that information. Please understand that Gregory and I are working hard to get to the bottom of it."

"Which is why it's so important for you to try and get that email Kenzie supposedly sent to Alex to me," Gregory told Ava. "The origins of that message could be the key to solving this case."

"Meaning it could finally prove once and for all that Collin is our culprit?" Ava asked.

"Exactly," Samantha confirmed.

Ava's cell phone buzzed. She dabbed the corners of her eyes with a napkin, then stared down at the screen.

"Oh no," she moaned. "My conference call started early. I need to get back to the office."

"Well, thanks for meeting with us," Samantha told her, "and for sharing that info about Kenzie."

"Yes, thank you, Ava," Gregory added while tapping his pen against the table.

"You're both welcome. And, uh… Detective Harris? I apologize for snapping at you the way I did. It's just—I guess I…"

"I understand," he said as her voice trailed off. "But an apology isn't necessary. This is tough for you. That's why we're doing all that we can to solve your brother's murder and get to the bottom of these disappearances."

"And I truly appreciate it." Ava stood up and slung her red suede handbag over her shoulder. "I'll reach out as soon as I hear back from Hudson on that email."

"Hey," Samantha chimed in, "do you think Hudson would be willing to talk to me? I really need to connect with somebody who's on the inside at Westman's."

"I don't see why not. He's just as concerned about the deaths of Jacob and the rest of the factory workers as we are. At this point, Hudson's actually worried about his own safety, too. I'll find out when I ask him to forward that email to me."

"Great, thanks. And Ava? Be careful out here."

"I will," she replied softly, placing her hand on Samantha's shoulder. "You do the same. Now that we know what Collin's really got going on, that puts a totally different spin on all this. He's got a lot to lose. And knowing him, he'd do whatever it takes to hold on to it. I just can't believe Chief Wentworth is in on this with him. I've known that man all my life. He's always been a fool for his son, but...*damn*."

"I can't believe it, either," Gregory said. "One of the reasons I came to Gattenburg was to escape the corruption running rampant throughout the Chicago PD. So to find out what's going on here is beyond disheartening. But I will say this. I let the situation in Chicago get the best of me. I'm not going to let that happen here."

"Why not?" Ava asked. "What's the difference between Chicago and Gattenburg?"

"That situation in Chicago was way bigger than me. I would've been in too deep trying to fight the majority of my precinct, politicians, the mafia." He paused, turning to Samantha with a fiery look of determination in his eyes. "Besides, I have a vested interest in Gattenburg. I have something to prove by solving this case and too much to lose if I don't. In more ways than one..."

Samantha peered back at the detective. The intensity in his gaze told her that he was referring to more than just the crimes occurring throughout the town. The thought of him being this invested in the investigation for her sake moved Samantha to the point where she was left speechless.

"Well, I appreciate everything you're doing," Ava told Gregory just as her cell phone went off again. "I'd better get going. We'll talk soon."

"Take care, Ava," Gregory said.

"Talk to you soon." Samantha watched as Ava slunk out of the restaurant. She felt a sharp pull in her chest at the sight of her hunched back and distraught expression. She was becoming a shell of herself. It was clear that Jacob's unsolved murder was eating away at her.

Samantha slid her hand across the table and gently

placed it on Gregory's arm. When he covered her hand with his, a jolt of tingling energy charged up her arm.

"Thank you so much for coming today," she told him. "I hope you know how much I appreciate you being here with me throughout all this madness. You don't have to help me, especially considering how this case has become such a conflict of interest for you. Yet you still choose to do so anyway. That really means a lot to me."

"I'm happy to help, but thank you for saying that. Judging from all this new information that continues to pour in," he said while flipping through his notepad, "we've got our work cut out for us."

"Yes, we do, starting with getting inside Westman's Automotive Factory."

Gregory ignored Samantha's suggestion. He polished off the rest of his coffee, then pushed away from the table.

"This was a good meeting," he said. "And helpful. Thanks for inviting me. But before this conversation takes a turn for the worst, I'd better get back to the station."

"Oh, so it's like that?" Samantha asked, watching as he stood up.

"Yes, Sam. It's like that. I'm not about to entertain the idea of breaking into Westman's. You already know how I feel about that. For now, I'm gonna focus on whether a missing-persons report has been filed on Kenzie. Then I'm going to reach out to my IT forensics guy and give him a heads-up on that email we're hoping to get from Ava. I'll be looking into the other drug busts, too, like I'd mentioned. I'm curious to see whether any patterns will emerge."

Samantha stood up and followed the detective toward the coffee shop's back door. She waved goodbye to Hannah and walked out into the alleyway, where they'd parked their cars in hopes of not being detected.

"So let me ask you this," Samantha began. "Would you consider bringing Alex down to the station to question him about Kenzie's disappearance?"

"I would. First, it will be good for others to see me pursuing a suspect, to let them think I don't believe Collin or any Wentworth is involved. But also, just to eliminate Alex as a suspect. Because at this point, I do believe that Collin is one hundred percent responsible for Kenzie's disappearance along with the rest of these crimes. Now it's just a matter of gathering enough evidence to take to the mayor."

"That was my exact thought when I asked the question. Get Alex alibied and out of the way so that we can focus on bringing charges against Collin."

Samantha paused, watching as Gregory clicked his key fob. Despite the unfortunate circumstances they were meeting under, she found herself not wanting to leave.

"By the way," he said, "I meant to tell you that my IT guy is back in Chicago. So there won't be any sort of conflict of interest when I ask him to look at the origins of that email."

"Oh, so you caught that look of concern on my face when you mentioned him earlier?" Samantha asked, smiling at the unspoken connection she and the detective shared.

"I did. But we got sidetracked when the subject of Collin's drug operation came up. So I just wanted you to know that we're good on that end."

"Awesome. Glad to hear it."

The pair stared at one another, neither of them wanting to part ways.

"All right then," Samantha finally said after several moments of silence. "Talk to you soon."

"Talk to you soon. Oh, I've meaning to ask you, has the patrol car been showing up and keeping watch on your house?"

"It sure has. Thank you again for getting that set up."

"No problem," Gregory told her. "Call me if you need me."

"I will. Thanks."

Samantha climbed inside her car and pulled out of the alleyway. On the way home, her thoughts shifted from Gregory to the dire situation at hand.

Now that Kenzie was missing and they knew for a fact that Collin was manufacturing dangerous drugs, her concern for the entire town was at an all-time high.

And although Gregory was completely against it, Samantha knew she had to figure out a way to get inside Westman's Automotive Factory.

Chapter Twelve

Gregory looked up from his desk through the open door of his small office. Chief Wentworth was walking around the precinct, sipping a cup of coffee while chatting with police officers scattered around the floor. The sight of him acting as if he didn't have a care in the world, as if he wasn't involved in Collin's drug operation, turned his stomach.

After searching several missing-persons databases, from the Illinois clearinghouse to all four federal systems, Gregory discovered that Kenzie's family hadn't reported her missing. He assumed they'd fallen for the email message she'd allegedly sent to Alex.

The detective had also begun digging through old drug files. But so far, there was no connection between them and his current investigation.

Just as he refreshed his email inbox yet again to see whether there were any new messages, his cell phone buzzed. He glanced over at the screen. Seeing Samantha's name caused a string of rapid-fire palpitations to explode inside his chest.

Dude, calm down...

"Detective Harris," he said coolly, acting as if he didn't know who it was.

"Hey, Gregory, it's Sam."

"Hey, what's going on?"

"I come bearing gifts."

"Do you now? What've you got for me?"

"I just received the email from Ava."

Gregory jumped up from behind his desk and closed the door. "Wait, you mean you got *the* email from Ava?"

"Yep. Hudson was able to talk Alex into sending it to him, and he passed it on to Ava."

"That is fantastic," he said, hurrying back to his desk and opening his laptop. "I need you to forward it to my personal email address."

"I'm sending it right now. And while I do that, let me tell you this. Ava found out from Hudson that he actually tried some of the drugs that Collin is manufacturing."

"Really? Wow. I wonder whether he's a recreational user or a full-blown addict."

"According to Hudson, he's a *former* addict. Jacob was the one who encouraged him to get clean and recommended him for the job at Westman's. He was hired, and after he completed the one-week second-chance program, one of his assembly team members at the factory invited him out to celebrate."

Gregory groaned and dropped his head in his hand. "I already know where you're going with this. But go on."

"At one point during their night out, the guy tempted Hudson with a drug he promised would be stronger than any black tar or street heroin he'd ever tried. He called it TKO."

"TKO, huh. Because of its ability to knock people out, I'm assuming?"

"You got it."

"Clever," Gregory snarked. "Do you know whether Hudson happened to mention the guy's name he was out with?"

"Nope. According to Ava, he refused to snitch."

"Of course..."

"So anyway, after Hudson took the drug, he OD'd and woke up in the hospital the next day. Couldn't remember a thing."

"Well, you and I saw that crazy list of ingredients in Collin's ledger. So hearing that someone OD'd on his product comes as no surprise."

Gregory once again refreshed his email inbox. Samantha's message from Hudson popped up.

"Hey, your email just came through. I've got my IT guy, Wayne, on standby. I'm shooting it over to him right now."

"Good. I can't wait to hear what he comes up with. Oh, and Ava was able to convince Hudson to talk to me. I'll see how much information I can get out of him. And I'm going to suggest we sit down and talk in person. I think a face-to-face would be more effective than a phone call."

"I agree. I always get way more information out of people in person than I do over the phone or via email. I wonder if he'd be open to me being there as well."

"I'm not sure. My gut tells me that the prospect of talking to a detective might turn him off. But I can certainly ask."

"Cool. Make sure you let him know that you and I are on the same team."

"I will."

When the pair grew silent, Gregory began fidgeting with a stack of papers sitting on his desk. He felt himself growing anxious. The detective realized it was because the conversation with Samantha was winding down, and he didn't want the call to end. He also wanted to do more, to protect her. He didn't like the thought of her doing these meet-ups alone.

At what point did you let your guard down and get this attached? he asked himself.

"So, um," Gregory continued, "do you think we should get together and discuss our next moves, aside from waiting on Wayne's analysis of the email?"

His knees bounced rapidly as he awaited her response.

"Yes, I think that's a good idea," Samantha replied without hesitation. "As a matter of fact, we can meet up at my place. I never did make that dinner for you that I promised."

Gregory sat back in his chair and grinned widely before pumping his fist in the air. "You most certainly didn't. And if I recall correctly, you were planning on cooking something up that would outdo the meal I prepared for you."

"Hold up now. I don't think I said all that," she laughed.

"Uh-uh, don't try and back out now. You said what you said. Now be a woman of your word and show me what you're working with. In the kitchen, that is," he quickly added.

"Oh, I'll show you what I'm working with all right," Samantha murmured. "Actually, I'm free tonight. If you're available, let's make it happen."

Gregory shifted in his seat, unable to stave off a

feeling of arousal so strong that it had him gripping the sides of his desk. "Let's do it."

"Great. I'll run by the grocery store and pick up a few things. See you at my place at around seven or so?"

"Seven works for me. How about I bring the wine?"

"Sounds perfect. See you tonight."

"See you then."

Just as Gregory pulled the phone away from his ear, Samantha called out his name.

"Hey! Before you go…" she said, her tone filled with mischief.

"What's up?"

"I know you've been really busy, but have you checked out my blog lately?"

"Not in the past few days. Why? Did I miss something?"

"Yes, you did. You missed a lot, actually."

"Uh-oh," Gregory uttered, pulling his laptop in closer and typing the web address for *Someone Knows Something* in the internet's search engine. "What are you up to now, Miss Vincent?"

"Let's just say I'm trying to shake things up around this town and bring more awareness to Collin and his drug ring. I want answers, Gregory. And I want Collin, his cronies and Chief Wentworth to be brought to justice. Clearly some of our police force is corrupt. You know several of them are probably being bribed and profiting off Collin's operation. So I'm using *Someone Knows Something* to call them out."

The detective sat silently for a moment, clenching his jaw while searching for the right thing to say. "Listen, Sam. I need you to be cautious. And low-key. Things are getting more and more dangerous out here. You don't want to draw too much attention to yourself right now."

He cringed when she sighed, frustrated, into the phone.

"That's not my intention," she insisted. "But we're getting so close to cracking this case. I don't wanna let up. The fact that Jacob's investigation went cold and authorities aren't looking further into the deaths of the Westman's workers is making me sick."

"I know it is. It's making me sick, too. That's why you and I are doing all that we can to build a strong case against Collin and Chief Wentworth to present to the district attorney. But I'm only going to get one shot at this, so I have to make sure my reporting is flawless. We just have to be patient and stay the course. Let my IT forensics guy figure out the origins of Kenzie's alleged email. Get everything we learned from Ava, Kenzie and Hudson officially recorded in a written statement. And turn over Collin's drug ledger—even if they can't use it at trial, it might still help."

"*And* share with the district attorney our findings once we get inside Westman's Automotive Factory and figure out what's really going on in there. I want photographic evidence of the drug lab that I am convinced is set up somewhere in that factory—"

"*Samantha,*" Gregory interrupted, the bark in his voice immediately silencing her. "Listen to me. There will be no breaking into Westman's Automotive Factory. Did you suddenly forget what happened when you broke into Collin's house? You almost got yourself killed!"

"But I didn't get—"

"This is not up for debate, dammit!" Gregory hollered, pounding the desk so loudly that several of his colleagues peered through the window on the door into his office. The detective held up his hand, letting them know that everything was okay. "Now, I'm serious," he continued into the phone, this time lowering his voice. "I don't want anything to happen to you, Samantha. Can't you understand that?"

"Yes," she replied quietly. "I do understand that."

Gregory's intense reaction to Samantha caused his throat to tighten. He could tell by her low tone that he'd rattled her. Knowing how resolute she could be, he knew that wasn't a bad thing.

"I don't want to press the issue," Samantha continued, "but I also don't want the DA's office to find some sort of loophole that would enable Collin and his father to get away with this. We need to have all the evidence we can get our hands on when you go to speak to him. Photographic proof would be the nail in their coffin."

"Well, I don't want you to end up *inside* a coffin trying to obtain that photographic evidence," Gregory shot back. "We'll have enough proof. Trust me. Proof that will stand up in court."

"I wonder if you could somehow get a warrant to search the factory."

Gregory couldn't help but chuckle at her tenacity. "You just aren't gonna let up, are you?"

"Nope."

"Well, I don't know about obtaining a warrant. But in the meantime, I'll continue to focus on what I am able to get my hands on."

"You do that. And I'll focus on getting to the grocery store so I can get started on this delicious dinner I'm about to cook up for you."

Hearing that caused the detective's stress level to

drop from ten to one. "That sounds good. I'm looking forward to it."

"So am I. See you soon."

"See you soon. Bye."

Gregory disconnected the call and reclined in his chair, folding his hands behind his head. He closed his eyes, his lips curling into a crooked grin at the thought of dinner with Samantha.

But when visions of intimate moments on the couch next to her over wine and deep conversation crept into his mind, his eyes popped open.

"Come on, man," he grumbled, sitting straight up. "Stay focused…"

He refreshed his email inbox. A message appeared from his computer forensics expert.

What's up, man. Just wanted to confirm that I received your email. I'll run an analysis on it and see if I can locate the server name and IP address. From there, I should be able to track down the owner and his/her location. If I have any trouble, I'll reach out to the internet service provider. You already know I've got the hookup with them, so I won't have to go through any red tape or present a warrant if I need to request additional information. I'll circle back with you once I know more.
Thanks,
Wayne

"My dude," Gregory said, slamming his hand down on the desk victoriously. He replied to Wayne's message and thanked him, then forwarded the email to Samantha.

We're well on our way to getting to the bottom of all this, he wrote before sending it.

When he heard a commotion outside his office, Gregory looked up and saw Chief Wentworth walking back into his office.

Gregory was tempted to go ask him if he'd had a chance to look over the police reports that were filed on the vandalisms at Samantha's house. But considering the new intel he had on the chief and his connection to Collin's drug ring, the detective decided against it. The last thing he wanted was to bring attention to himself and Samantha and cause a disruption in their investigation.

Follow your own advice, he told himself. *Just be patient and stay the course.*

And with that, Gregory pulled Samantha's blog back up and began reading her latest post, which she'd aptly titled "We're Getting Closer to the Truth, My Friends…"

Chapter Thirteen

By the time Samantha walked out of the grocery store, darkness had already fallen over the town. She peered into the parking lot in search of her car. When it didn't immediately come into view, she clicked on the key fob until taillights blinked over in the far right corner.

Samantha glanced around the lot before stepping out onto the asphalt. There were very few cars scattered about between the neon-yellow lines. Most of the townspeople usually did their grocery shopping on the weekends, including her. But since her impromptu dinner with Gregory was planned at the last minute, she had no choice but to make a last-minute run to the store.

"Shoot," Samantha muttered when one of the handles on her shopping bag tore. She bent down and grabbed the steaks and potatoes before they went tumbling to the ground.

Just as she gathered the top of the bag and twisted it into a knot, the sound of a revving engine roared behind her.

A stinging cloud of dread seeped through Samantha's pores. Her entire body stiffened up. She looked ahead at her car, her vision blurring with fear. It appeared to be miles away.

"Please, please, please," she begged, willing her heavy feet to lift off the ground and get her to the vehicle. But it was as if she were in the midst of a nightmare. Everything around her began to move in slow motion and she was stuck in one spot, literally unable to budge.

But when the sound of screeching tires pierced her ears, she let out a loud scream and darted through the parking lot.

Samantha refused to look behind her for fear that it would slow her down. When she reached her car, she fell onto the trunk trying to get around to the driver's side.

"Come on," she whimpered, clutching her bags tighter. "Come on!"

The heel of her boot slipped into a crack in the asphalt. Samantha fumbled, gripping the bumper on the back of her car while barely avoiding falling to the ground.

Get up, get up, get up!

She scrambled to her feet, shuddering as a gust of blustering wind rushed past her.

Samantha whipped around and was blinded by bright yellow headlights. A car was careening toward her at full speed.

Once again, she found herself unable to move. A stiffening shock invaded her limbs. Her body felt as though it was cemented to the ground.

As the car zoomed closer toward her, Samantha realized that it was the same dark sedan she'd seen in the alleyway the night her garage was vandalized.

Her eyes widened with terror. She struggled to peer inside the windows to see who was behind the wheel. But she couldn't see through the dark tint.

Samantha recoiled against the back of her car as the vehicle raced past her. She dropped her grocery bags and screamed in terror. The car tore through the lot and onto the street then disappeared into the night.

"Ma'am!" a woman yelled as she ran toward Samantha. "Are you all right?"

Samantha clung to the back of her car, trembling with fear as tears streamed down her face.

"I… I think so," she stammered, her shaky voice indicating that she was far from okay.

She watched as a woman scurried past her and picked her groceries up off the ground.

"I saw what just happened to you," the woman said, reaching down and helping Samantha stand up straight. "What was with the crazy driver of that car?"

"It's a long story," Samantha sighed. She patted her damp face with the sleeve of her coat, then took her bags from the woman. "Thank you so much."

Samantha spun around and rushed inside her car. Her hands struggled to grip her phone and dial Gregory's number. When she finally got the call to go through, he picked up on the first ring.

"Hey, I was just thinking about you," he said. "I'm really looking forward to our dinner tonight."

Before Samantha could say a word, she burst into tears.

"Wh-what's going on?" he asked. "Are you crying?"

"I'm at the grocery store," she sobbed, "and when I came out into the parking lot, somebody tried to run me over!"

"Wait, somebody *what*?"

"Somebody tried to hit me with their car!" she cried out, clenching her heaving chest.

"Okay, calm down," the detective said soothingly. "Are you still at the store?"

Samantha could hear him rustling about, then heard a door slam. A feeling of relief rushed over her knowing he was already on his way there.

"Yes. I'm in the parking lot. But I don't feel safe staying here. At all."

"Okay. Why don't you head to your house and I'll meet you there? The squad car should be watching over your place. At this point, though, I'm honestly not comfortable with the idea of you staying in your home. If it's okay with you, I'd like you to pack a bag and come stay with me."

Samantha opened her mouth to speak, but she couldn't even formulate the words to express how thankful she was for Gregory.

"Are you still there?" he asked after several moments of silence. "I hope that suggestion didn't make you uncomfortable."

"No, it didn't," she whispered. "Not at all. That's extremely generous of you to offer. And I will take you up on it. Thank you."

Samantha started her car and pulled out of the lot. Her head swiveled back and forth as she searched for the dark sedan, afraid that it would come flying at her out of nowhere. But the street was empty.

"I'm on my way to your place now," Gregory told her. "I'll stay on the phone with you until you get there."

"Thanks," she replied, a rush of gratitude managing to overpower the burning fear churning throughout her body.

"No problem. I know you're tough and all, but what

you went through tonight must have been terrifying. I'm so sorry this is all happening to you, Samantha."

"I'm scared, Gregory," she blurted out in spite of hating to admit it. She wasn't used to feeling this vulnerable. But no cold case she'd ever covered had hit this close to home, to the point where she was in such danger.

"I know you are, Sam. I clearly need to step up protecting you. The good news is that we're closing in on Collin. The bad news is, he knows it. So he's amping up the threat against you in hopes that you'll back off. If it's any consolation, he's unlikely to do anything in such a public place. He wants to scare you enough that you'll stop investigating."

Samantha felt a streak of anger shoot through her. She squeezed the steering wheel and pressed down on the accelerator.

"That'll never happen," she insisted. "I don't give a damn how scared I am, or how crazy Collin gets. I refuse to let up until he is behind bars. *Period.* I will not quit until we get justice for Jacob."

"I understand that, Sam. But like I keep telling you, you can't risk losing your life over this. Maybe you should let up on the blog posts for now. Go dark for a minute. Let him think you backed off. Focus on the results we're waiting to get back from my IT forensics guy. We've also got Hudson on our team now. Have you tried to set up that meeting with him?"

"I did. I reached out to him earlier this afternoon. I'm just waiting to hear back."

"Okay, good. Hopefully you'll hear back soon."

The pair grew silent for several seconds. Samantha

could feel the pressure as the situation began to close in on them.

Yet as thoughts of staying at Gregory's place crossed her mind, she realized that it was all bringing them closer together.

"I'm a few blocks away from your house now," he told her. "How far away are you?"

"I should be there in a couple of minutes."

"Okay. I want you to pull your car into the garage—"

"Which I did get fixed, by the way," Samantha interjected.

"Glad to hear it. Once you pull your car in, I'll go inside the house with you while you pack a bag. Move as quickly as you can, grab what you need, then we'll take my car back to my house. Cool?"

"Sounds good. Oh, and I'm so sorry about dinner. You have Collin to blame for missing out on the filet mignon, double-baked potatoes and grilled asparagus I was planning on preparing tonight."

"Do you really think I'm about to let Collin ruin our dinner plans? I still have every intention of indulging in our meal. We'll just pull a little switch up and I'll take the reins and whip up the meal for us. I've got a fantastic red wine that'll go well with those steaks you bought, too."

"You're so good to me. That would be wonderful. I could really go for a glass of wine right about now. Or three…"

"Well, lucky for you I've got a couple of bottles," Gregory laughed. "And I just bought a new set of furniture for my deck. Why don't we sit out there and eat? I can cook up the steaks on the grill, light up the heat lamps and fire pit. Then after we enjoy a nice, relaxing meal, we'll plot out our next moves on gathering the evidence to present to Mayor Elliot."

Samantha felt her stiff back slacken as Detective Harris put her at ease. "I'd like that. We can do it over the cheesecake I bought for dessert."

"Mmm, now my mouth is watering…"

When she turned down her block, Samantha was relieved to see Gregory's car parked in front of her house.

"By the way," he said, "I just pulled up in front of your house."

"I see you. I'm pulling up now."

Samantha drove up beside Gregory, waving as he nodded and waved back. She could tell by the look in his shining eyes that he was just as pleased to see her as she was him. She lowered the window.

"Thank you so much for coming to my rescue yet again," Samantha told him.

"Ah, don't even mention it. At this point you're working harder for the Gattenburg PD than our actual employees. I consider you one of us now. Therefore, I owe it to you to look out."

"I appreciate you."

"It's my pleasure…"

The twosome sat there gazing at one another before Samantha noticed the squad car that'd been keeping watch over her house blink its headlights at her. She tapped her horn and waved.

"I'm really grateful that Officer Barris has been keeping an eye on my house. Thanks again for setting that up."

"No problem." The detective shifted in his seat and glanced behind him. "All right. Enough with the small talk. We'll have plenty of time for that once we get to my place. Why don't you go ahead and pull into the garage, then grab your things? I'll meet you at the front door."

"Will do."

Samantha turned into her driveway and clicked the garage door opener. As she waited for the door to rise, she glanced in her rearview mirror and watched as Gregory stepped out of his car.

He threw on his black leather motorcycle jacket while strolling toward her front door. The cool, confident swagger in his gait, mixed with his sexy good looks and gym-honed physique, had her wondering how she would get through staying at his house without slipping out of her bed and into his.

"Gregory, this was absolutely delicious," Samantha said, dabbing the corners of her mouth with her napkin. "I hate to admit it, but my meal probably wouldn't have been as good as yours."

"Nonsense. Stop trying to boost my self-esteem. I'm sure yours would've been better."

Samantha felt a tingling heat creep up the back of her neck underneath the intensity of Gregory's gaze. She picked up her glass of cabernet and took a long sip, focusing on the rim as opposed to his seductive stare. She knew that if she looked him directly in the eye, she just might jump across the table and do something wildly inappropriate.

"Well," she continued, discreetly patting away the beads of sweat that had formed along her hairline, "the filet mignon was grilled to perfection. The twice-baked potatoes were crispy on the outside and nice and tender on the inside, just like I like them. And the charred grilled asparagus was tender and full of flavor."

Gregory's lips spread into a gradual smile. Samantha pressed her fingertips against her mouth and threw him a chef's kiss.

"My compliments to the chef. This was amazing."

"Why, thank you. You know what they say—when you cook with love in your heart, the meal is always delicious."

Samantha cocked her head to one side and felt herself swoon at the sound of those words. "That is what they say, isn't it?"

"It is…"

Gregory refilled their glasses, then set the bottle back down, his expression growing somber. "So, I've tried to avoid talking about what happened to you tonight for as long as I possibly could, but we do need to discuss it."

She swallowed hard as the elevated energy in her mood quickly spiraled upward. "I know we do. I'm okay. We can discuss it."

He swirled his wine around in the glass before continuing. "So you're sure the car that almost hit you is the same vehicle you saw in the alleyway the day your garage was vandalized?"

"Yes. I'm positive it was the same car."

"But neither you nor the woman who helped you today were able to get a good look at the license plate?"

"Unfortunately, no. We didn't. That would've been such a huge help, too."

"It would have. But that's okay. I've been trying to keep an eye out on all the dark sedans I see across town and run their license plate numbers. My plan is to pull them over and ask questions if anything suspect comes up in the system. So far, they've all turned up clean."

"Humph. Well, hopefully something will turn up soon. We know Collin drives that obnoxious pickup truck, so my guess is that it's one of his boys."

"That's my guess, too."

Gregory took a swallow of wine, then leaned back in his chair. "Listen, I really hope you took what I mentioned earlier to heart. I want you to start keeping a low profile. Not only should you go dark on the blog for a while, but start being more low-key around town, too. I'll continue to have Officer Barris keep an eye out on your house. Now that we see Collin and his associates are playing dirtier, we'll be keeping a closer eye on you, too."

The thought of being confined and having to watch her every move irritated Samantha to her core. But deep down, she knew the detective was looking out for her best interest.

"Okay," she reluctantly agreed. "I can do that."

"You can?" he asked, sounding surprised. "That's it? You're not gonna give me any type of pushback?"

"Nope—" she shrugged "—because I know you're right. I may be tenacious, but I'm not stupid. It's obvious that Collin is willing to do whatever he can to silence me. I've seen firsthand what's come of Jacob and the other factory workers. I don't want to suffer the same fate."

"And I don't want you to. So I'm glad we're on the same page."

Samantha took several sips of wine while staring thoughtfully into the flames flickering in the fire pit. "At this point, I know that getting Mayor Elliot involved is our best hope. So I'm willing to stand down while we gather the necessary evidence to present to him."

Gregory held his hand up and gave Samantha a high five. "It's so awesome to hear you say that, *partner.*"

"And it's so awesome to hear you call me partner. Remember back when you wouldn't even talk to me about this investigation? Look at you now."

He chuckled self-consciously. "Yeah, well, what can I say? You presented a pretty compelling case. Then you charmed me with your good looks and alluring personality. So technically I had no choice."

"Oh, is that what I did?" Samantha laughed.

"It sure is."

The twosome stared at each other across the table. Through the corner of her eye, Samantha noticed Gregory's hand slowly sliding toward hers. Just as their fingertips touched, the heat lamp above them went out.

"Oh no," he muttered, glancing up at it. When he stood up and tinkered with the on/off switch, the fire pit's flames began to die down.

"What is happening right now?" Samantha asked.

"I know, right? Are our heat sources trying to tell us something?"

"Yeah, that we need to wrap things up out here and go back inside," she told him.

"Maybe so. Because it looks like this heat lamp is out for the count. I just bought this thing, too. Oh well, it'll be going right back to the store tomorrow."

As Gregory poured water over the fire pit to snuff out the remaining flames, Samantha stood up and began collecting their dishes.

"By the way," she said, "since I didn't hear back from

Hudson, I sent him another text message asking if he'd be willing to talk with me tomorrow."

"Good. Hopefully he'll say yes, then offer up some pertinent information to add to the file we're building for Mayor Elliot." The detective paused, staring at Samantha thoughtfully. "But I don't know. After what happened tonight in that parking lot, I don't want you meeting with Hudson in person. It could be dangerous if you two are seen together. Try and make it either a phone call or video chat."

Samantha slid the patio door open, then turned to Gregory and nodded her head. "I think that's a good idea. Better safe than sorry."

She paused, contemplating her next thought before continuing. "Hey, there's something else that's been on my mind. I know you want me to be low-key moving forward and all, but I really want to share what happened to me tonight with Ava. She needs to be careful out here, too. Everybody in town knows she's working to get justice for Jacob, which means she could possibly be in danger. Wouldn't you agree?"

"Yes, I definitely agree. No one involved in this case can be too careful at this point." Gregory grabbed the rest of the dishes and followed Samantha inside. He set everything in the sink then turned to her. "You know what? I'm going to fill out a police report and take a statement from you on what happened in that parking lot tonight."

"Don't you think that'll draw unwanted attention to us?"

"I do. Which is why I'm not going to actually process the report. I'm just going to fill it out and add it to the file that we're building for the district attorney, along with the vandalism reports on your house that I actually did process."

"You mean the ones that Chief Wentworth promised to look into then completely forgot about?"

"Yes, those," Gregory chortled, pulling the cheesecake from the refrigerator and placing it on the counter. "I just need the mayor to have a record of every incident and each piece of evidence we've gathered. That should make it easy for him to draw up charges against Collin, Chief Wentworth and everyone else involved in the drug ring."

"Speaking of everyone else, did you find any reports on drug busts that may be linked to Westman's?"

"Only one. It involved a temporary employee who worked there briefly during the summer. He nearly OD'd after a night out with several of the assembly workers."

"Let me guess. No charges were ever filed against anyone."

"Unfortunately, no," Gregory sighed. "I did some digging into Chief Wentworth's background, too. I expected to find evidence of him using that drug money to make major purchases, take lavish vacations, something. But surprisingly, he lives a pretty modest lifestyle."

"Hmm, interesting. Maybe he pays for everything with cash and keeps his toys stashed away in another town."

"Maybe…"

Samantha poured the last of the wine into their glasses and handed one to Gregory. After they each took a sip, he reached over and covered her hand with his. "So how are you feeling now? Are you all right?"

"I'm still a bit shaken up." She shrugged. "But being here with you is certainly helping to keep me calm."

He caressed her hand while gazing at her sympathetically. Samantha responded by intertwining her fingers within his.

When he began stroking her palm with his thumb, the arousing sensation caused a nagging voice to go off inside her head.

Don't get distracted before you complete your mission...

She cleared her throat and slipped her hand from his grip. "So anyway," she continued, "thank you for tonight. Especially that delicious meal."

The detective paused, as if surprised by the abrupt way in which she disrupted their intimate moment and changed the subject.

"I'm glad you enjoyed it," he told her. "Are you ready for dessert?"

"I am. I'll grab a couple of plates and forks."

Gregory pulled a can of whipped cream and a container of mixed berries out of the refrigerator. "Look what I've got."

"Ooh, nice. Those'll go great with the cheesecake."

"I thought so, too."

He cut two slices of cake and slid them onto the plates, then topped them with the garnishes.

"I'll tell you what," Gregory continued. "Why don't we take our dessert and wine into the television room and get lost in some trashy reality TV show? No more talk of Collin, Chief Wentworth or their drug operation. Let's just decompress and enjoy the rest of the evening together. How does that sound?"

"That sounds perfect."

Samantha trailed behind Gregory as he led her down a hallway into the den. The pair got comfy on his chocolate-brown leather couch while he grabbed the remote and turned on the television.

"So look," she told him, "I'm not trying to watch anything pertaining to sports or pimped-out hot rods."

"Well, I'm not trying to watch any makeup or modeling competitions."

"Awfully presumptuous, aren't you?"

"Aren't *you*?" Gregory rebutted before they both burst out laughing.

"Listen, why don't we find some middle ground here? What about *90 Day Fiancé*?"

"Ninety day what?"

"90 Day Fiancé!" Samantha repeated. "It's this crazy reality show about people in the United States who connect with foreigners overseas."

Gregory shook his head while punching buttons on the remote. "Okay, that sounds absolutely insane."

"Yeah, but I see you're doing a search for it, so obviously you're interested."

"Obviously," he retorted before nudging Samantha's arm. "Found it. Let me see what this madness is all about…"

As Gregory hit the play button, Samantha reclined farther back into the couch and slid a piece of cheesecake inside her mouth. While her day had been traumatic, she was overcome by a sense of peace and protection being in the detective's presence.

But in the back of her mind, Samantha had an uneasy feeling that the worst was yet to come.

Chapter Fourteen

Gregory glanced down at his watch. It was a little after three o'clock in the afternoon. He was still at the station, refreshing his personal email inbox like a madman.

His IT forensics guy, Wayne, had promised he'd get back to him with some answers on Kenzie's email before the end of the workday. But the detective still hadn't heard from him.

Gregory had been able to schedule a last-minute appointment with the district attorney at four o'clock that afternoon. He was eager to report on Wayne's findings, along with the information that he and Samantha had gathered.

"Come on, dammit," Gregory grumbled, once again pounding the touchpad on his laptop. Still no new messages.

Just as he pushed away from the desk, his cell phone rang.

"Detective Harris," he barked without even checking the caller ID.

"Hey, is everything okay?"

The sound of Samantha's voice on the other end of the phone quickly put Gregory at ease.

"Hey, yeah, everything's okay. Well, actually, no.

It's isn't. I thought I would've heard back from Wayne by now regarding Kenzie's email. I'm getting worried, because it's been radio silence on his end. I hope this isn't gonna end up being one of the rare cases where he's unable to track the message."

"Well, the day isn't over yet. So just relax and give him a little more time. Maybe Collin was smart enough to send the email through a virtual private network rather than his own internet service provider. If so, its origins would be harder to trace. Either way, I'm sure you'll hear back from Wayne with some news soon."

Gregory gnawed at his thumbnail. "I hope you're right. I'm just feeling an immense amount of pressure because we're running out of time here. We've got to get this report to the DA before Collin strikes again. I don't want anybody else to turn up missing, or dead, or worse. Especially you…"

He paused and took a deep breath, unable to go on.

"Just breathe, Gregory," Samantha said calmly. "You're good. *We're* good. We are making some great strides here. Don't start letting this case get the best of you. We've come too far to break down now. According to you, Wayne is a pro, right?"

"Yes, he is."

"And he's never failed you before, has he?"

"No," Gregory sighed, falling back in his chair and taking a long sip of stale, lukewarm coffee. "He hasn't."

"Well, trust and believe that he isn't going to let you down now. I know the clock is ticking. But let's just be patient. Wayne will come through for you soon enough."

The detective rubbed his burning eyes. Between worrying about their investigation and fighting off sensual thoughts of Samantha all night as she slept in the room right next to his, he hadn't gotten much rest.

"Now," she continued, "the reason why I'm calling is because I've got some pretty explosive news to share with you."

"You do?" Gregory hopped up and closed the door when he noticed several police officers gathering near his office. "All right, let's hear it."

"I spoke with Hud—"

"Wait, hold up a sec," the detective interrupted when he heard his computer ping.

He rushed back over to the desk and refreshed his email inbox. A new message from Wayne appeared on the screen.

"Bingo!" he yelled so loudly that the officers standing outside his office peered at him through the glass window with raised eyebrows.

Gregory threw them a thumbs-up, indicating that all was well before turning back to his computer.

"What is going on?" Samantha asked.

"I just got an email from Wayne."

"See! I told you he wouldn't let you down. What does it say?"

He rolled his chair up to the desk and clicked on the message.

"It says, 'What's up, man, sorry it took me a minute to get back to you. I got the results back on the email. It was sent through a VPN rather than an ISP, so tracking the sender's IP address was a challenge. But what the sender didn't realize is that some VPNs keep a record of users' internet movement. So I was able to log the server activity, hence enabling me to trace him.'"

"Got it. Now come on. Get to the good part!" Samantha insisted.

"Okay, okay," the detective said, "The last paragraph says, 'So you were right, the IP address that I traced the email back to belongs to Collin Wentworth.'"

Gregory heard Samantha gasp as she realized what this meant. Collin must have used Kenzie's email address to send the message, but he'd done it from his own IP address.

"Wow," she breathed. "We called it. You and I both knew Collin was behind that message. But hearing the confirmation from an expert is wonderful. Everything is really falling into place with this case."

"I know, right? I only wish we'd gotten the info we needed before Kenzie disappeared," the detective said as he printed out Wayne's message and added it to his file for the district attorney.

"I know. But we're doing what we can as fast as we can. And I haven't even told you what I found out from Hudson when we spoke today."

"Wait, you talked to Hudson?"

"Yes! That's what I was about to tell you when Wayne's email came through. Listen, he spilled all types of tea on Collin, his drug ring *and* the deceased Westman's workers."

Gregory looked up and noticed that the cops milling around his office seemed to be doing more than just chatting among themselves. It appeared as though they were trying to eavesdrop on his conversation.

"Hey, hold that thought," he told Samantha before lowering his voice. "There are some officers congregating outside my office, and I don't know what they're up to. So why don't we continue this conversation after I leave the station?"

"Good idea. Because we don't know who's on whose team in there. Better safe than sorry."

"Exactly." Gregory kept his eyes on the window of his office while grabbing his laptop and car key. "Listen, I know you've been cooped up in my house all day. After my meeting with the DA, why don't I come pick you up and we'll go grab some sushi for dinner? There's a new spot that just opened up over on Spranton. I hear it's pretty private and low-key. I highly doubt that we'll be spotted in that area."

"Mmm, sushi would be delicious. I'm actually in the middle of clawing my way through an article for the women's journal on how to manage your anxiety when life gets too overwhelming. Needless to say, I could use a break."

"So basically working on a piece that sums up everything you're going through right now."

"Exactly."

Gregory got up and opened his office door. The cops standing nearby quickly stepped to the side, their tense expressions appearing apprehensive. The detective acknowledged them with a slight nod, his blank stare more cold than friendly.

"These dudes are in here acting a little funny toward me," he muttered into the phone as he swaggered through the police station.

"I wonder how many of them know what their beloved Chief Wentworth is actually up to."

"Speaking of the devil…"

Gregory walked past the break room and noticed the chief holding court with Officers Baxter and Miller near the vending machine. They were cracking up laughing while toasting with soda cans and slapping one another on the backs.

"*Which* devil?" Samantha snarked. "Because there appear to be a whole lot of them in there."

"You're right. But this time I'm referring to Chief Wentworth and his cronies, Baxter and Miller," he said, keeping his voice low.

"You mean those two clowns who showed up to my house and conducted that half-ass investigation after Collin busted out my windows?"

Gregory subdued a laugh as he pushed through the station's revolving door and walked out into the parking lot.

"Yeah, those two."

"Well, hopefully your meeting with the district attorney will put an end to all this madness and these criminals will finally be charged with their crimes."

"That's my hope, too," the detective said as he climbed inside his car. "I'm feeling really confident now that we have proof of Kenzie's email being sent from Collin's IP address, along with all the other evidence we've gathered."

"Same here. And I'm looking forward to us making a toast over dinner to what I already know will be a fantastic meeting with the DA."

Gregory felt a surge of excitement at the thought of sharing an intimate dinner with Samantha unrelated to the case.

It had been a long time since he'd actually taken a woman out on a date. Memories of courting an ex-girlfriend back in Chicago came to mind. They'd spent countless nights together, sharing candlelit dinners in

Little Italy and dancing to jazz music in tiny clubs in Wicker Park.

Stop it, Gregory told himself, quickly pushing those thoughts out of his head. The last thing he wanted to do was compare what they had to his old life back in Chicago.

"Hey, you still there?" she asked, snapping him out of his thoughts.

"Yeah, I am. Sorry about that. What were you saying?"

"I was saying that I'm going to hang up so I can finish up some work, then start getting ready."

"Gotcha. I missed that. I was, uh…thinking about what types of sushi rolls I'm gonna order later," Gregory lied.

"Mmm, I'll have to go online and check out their menu. Good luck with the meeting, and I will be ready when you get here."

"Thanks. See you soon."

He disconnected the call and took a deep breath.

Keep your cool. And get your emotions in check… Detective Harris thought as he headed to the DA's office.

"I CANNOT BELIEVE I let you talk me into this," Gregory said, shaking his head as a feeling of regret took hold of him. He clutched the steering wheel while making a right turn onto Everhart Avenue, then slowly drove down the street.

"Trust me, we're doing the right thing," Samantha insisted. "This is the last piece of evidence that we need to hand over to the district attorney in order for him to file charges against Collin, Chief Wentworth and whoever else is involved in their drug ring."

Detective Harris tapped on the brake and pulled over when Westman's Automotive Factory came into view. He glanced down at the clock. It was a little after nine o'clock.

The pair had just left dinner. Gregory and Samantha had spent most of the evening discussing how his meeting with the district attorney went left after the DA insisted that the detective didn't have enough evidence to execute any warrants, let alone arrests.

Gregory decided against showing him Collin's drug ledger since it was obtained without a warrant, making it inadmissible to present as evidence in court.

After the detective and Samantha left the restaurant, she'd received a text message from Hudson. His friend was working security at Westman's and agreed to let them inside the factory after hours.

"So look," Samantha began, "according to Hudson, the maintenance crew is usually done cleaning at about nine o'clock. So we should be good."

"*We?* What do you mean we? I haven't agreed to step foot inside that factory with you. Now, for the thousandth time, this is a bad idea, Samantha. The DA isn't going to use anything you find here, so you could be jeopardizing any case we do end up putting together. And you're once again risking your life by breaking into this place in search of an alleged drug laboratory that you're not even sure exists!"

"But what if it does?" she shot back, her eyes dancing wildly as she stared across the street at Westman's. "That would be a slam dunk, *guaranteeing* a prison cell inside the Menard Correctional Center with Collin's and his father's names written on it."

"So you're envisioning them being sent to the toughest prison in the state, huh?"

Samantha threw her hands in the air and looked around in confusion. "Of course! With capital murder, kidnapping and drug trafficking charges against them, where else would they go?"

"True. But as for this second break-in you're trying to pull off? Don't do this. After we gather more evidence and present it to the DA, I'm sure he'll generate a search warrant so that the factory can be inspected legally."

"I'm not breaking in. The security guard is going to *let* me in. And I hear what you're saying, but I just can't pass up this opportunity, Gregory. Now, Hudson is already inside the factory. Should I text him back and let him know we're here?"

Gregory rubbed his eyes in frustration then stared out the window. Thoughts of all the various ways things could go wrong flooded his mind.

"I'm really looking for a way to talk you out of this," he said.

"Nothing you say can talk me out of this."

The detective shook his head in disbelief. "I cannot believe this is happening right now..." He turned his attention toward Westman's. "This security guard I see leaning against the wall eating a submarine sandwich, he's Hudson's boy?"

"Yes. And he was friends with Jacob, too. So he wants to see Collin get locked up just as badly as the rest of us. The only reason he's still working at Westman's is because he has a family to support."

A pang of doubt rattled inside Gregory's chest. "I'm telling you, Samantha. I am not feeling this. At all."

She rolled her eyes and slumped down in her seat.

"But," the detective continued, "with that being said, I can go in and meet with Hudson instead of you. It'd be too dangerous for—"

"No," Samantha interrupted. "Trust me. Hudson won't meet with you alone. I have to do this myself."

Gregory paused, watching as she slowly glanced over at him.

"I don't want a repeat of what happened during the incident at Collin's house, where you were all alone having to fend for yourself. While I may not agree with what you're doing here, my conscience won't allow me to let you do this by yourself. I'm an officer of the law. This meeting is with an informant. That will keep it aboveboard."

"Thank you, Gregory," she replied softly.

"Don't," he said. "Don't thank me. I'm not happy with this."

"Oh, come on," Samantha said. "You'll be thanking me when the district attorney presents the photos I'm about to take to the jury once Collin and Chief Wentworth go to trial."

"Let me handle any photos. Remember, it's a meeting with an informant. I take the lead," he said.

"You know what? I—"

Samantha was interrupted when her cell phone buzzed.

"Saved by the bell," she said before grabbing it off her lap and peering down at the screen. "That's Hudson texting me again. He said that if I'm coming to meet him over at the side door, because there's no security camera posted above the doorway."

Gregory looked up at the parking lot's back door and noticed a camera hovering over the entryway.

"He's just now figuring that out?" he asked, his words tinged with doubt.

Samantha ignored him. "Beechwood Street—that's where the side door entrance is located."

Without saying another word, Detective Harris took off, speeding down the street and around the corner. He drove in silence, his jaw set tight, his anger and apprehension growing.

Once at the Beechwood entrance, Gregory threw the car into Park and turned off the headlights.

Samantha stared at him with wide eyes filled with anger. "Can I expect you to still be here when I come out?" she asked curtly.

"I'm going in with you," he said, not looking at her.

"If you do that, Hudson will bolt."

"I told you—I take the lead. Or this isn't happening."

In response, she opened the door and got out. When he did the same, she turned and stopped.

"Don't. Don't come with me. I promise I'll be careful. I won't compromise the investigation. If you come with me, it's over."

It's over. The investigation or them?

Gregory pushed out a sigh. He knew Samantha would do this with or without him. He had to play by her rules now or deal with the fallout of her going at it alone when he wasn't around to protect her.

"Okay," he gritted out. "I trust you. Now you trust me. If I think you are in trouble, I will come in there. I made a commitment to look after you, and I'll honor it."

"Thank you," Samantha mumbled, her voice barely a whisper. She sent Hudson a message letting him know she was on her way inside.

Gregory stayed in the shadows and watched as she

approached the factory's steel-gray side door, every muscle and nerve in his body yelling at him to go after her. He stayed put, watching as the door opened just as she reached up to knock.

The detective craned his neck, trying to catch a glimpse of Hudson. But the bleak, dimly lit entryway was too dark for him to make out the figure standing on the doorstep. Within seconds, Samantha slipped inside and the door quickly slammed shut.

"Please don't let anything happen to this woman," Gregory said to himself, closing his eyes.

Thoughts of Samantha being confronted by Collin or getting hurt while inside the factory flooded his mind.

The detective's eyes flew open as a sense of urgency rushed through his body. He couldn't just stand here and wait. He had to do something.

His eyes were met with darkness. Only faint streams of light shone down on the desolate street in the distance from the scarce streetlights.

He pulled out his phone and composed a text message to Samantha.

Have Hudson send the security guard a text letting him know I'm going to be walking around outside the factory. I need to keep a closer eye on things. If you get the sense that something's wrong, get the hell out. I'll be here for you.

He sent the message, and without waiting for a reply, crept around to the side of the building, eyeing the old, thick, frosted windows lining the factory's lower level.

Gregory stooped down and leaned into one of the windows. He held his hands against the sides of his eyes, attempting to peer inside the building. But the cloudy haze covering the glass prevented him from seeing a thing.

He stood up and stepped away from the window, ignoring the stench of rotting food coming from a rusted-out nearby dumpster. A twinge of angst pulled at his chest as he anxiously waited to hear back from Samantha.

The detective pulled the phone from his back pocket, checking to see whether she'd texted him back. She hadn't.

"Don't start worrying," he told himself, struggling to ignore the sense of panic beginning to simmer inside his head.

When a frigid wind whipped past him, Gregory grabbed a black wool skull cap out of his coat pocket and slipped it over his head. Just as he reached for his black leather gloves, his cell phone buzzed. He exhaled with relief after a text message from Samantha popped up on the screen.

Hudson let the guard know you're on the scene. You're good. We're in the factory's overflow supply room now. It's on the lower level, northeast side. Hudson thinks there's some sort of secret entrance into the drug lab here. I'll keep you posted.

Good, Gregory wrote back. Don't stay too long. Leave if you don't find something soon. Otherwise, I'll come in.

After the detective sent the message, he pulled on his black leather gloves and scanned the area. There weren't many cars driving down the road. The only sounds he heard were the wind whistling past his ears and faint rumblings of a freight train in the distance.

He reached behind him and felt for the nine-millimeter he'd tucked away in the back of his jeans. It was still firmly in place, waiting to be drawn if necessary...

Chapter Fifteen

Samantha walked closely behind Hudson. She squinted her eyes in an attempt to see what was in front of her as they tiptoed through the huge, dimly lit supply room.

Very few of the industrial strip lights hanging from the high ceilings seemed to be working. Those that were flickered off and on sporadically like something from a horror movie, the effect enhanced by creepy buzzing sounds hissing underneath the lights' surface.

She tried to ignore the eerie chills crawling up her back and focus on Hudson's thick, shaggy red hair. But when she heard a loud thud bang against one of the windows, she gasped and practically leaped onto his scrawny back.

"What the hell was that?" she whispered.

"Who knows?" he replied nonchalantly, waving his hand in the air as if he didn't have a care in the world. "Probably just a cat or something. Let's just keep moving."

Samantha pursed her lips tightly together, forcing herself not to press the issue. Ava had forgotten to mention just how much of a burnout Hudson was. His drug abuse issues were obvious, from his small pupils and slurred speech to his gaunt appearance and constant scratching. Despite the fact that the factory's basement was freezing cold, Hudson was sweating profusely.

But Samantha was trying her best to ignore all that and stay focused on the goal. If she had to follow the lead of a drug addict in order to get Collin and Chief Wentworth behind bars, then so be it.

"It is so rancid in here," she whispered, covering her nose with her hand.

There wasn't a stream of air circulating through the dank room. Between its musty odor and the stench of sweat wafting off Hudson, Samantha felt as though she might gag.

"Let's just find what we're looking for so we can grab what we need and get the hell outta here," he mumbled, stomping his feet against the floor as if looking for a trap door.

Samantha side-eyed him suspiciously. She was beginning to wonder whether he was looking to score drugs inside Collin's lab as opposed to helping her gather evidence.

She pulled out her cell phone and turned on the flashlight, then held it up toward the steel shelving units on either side of her. They were packed with sheets of metal, heaps of plastics, boxes of rubber and stacks of fiberglass.

When they reached the end of the aisle, Hudson turned and headed down the next one while continuing to stomp the floor.

"Hey," she whispered, knowing they were the only two inside the factory but still feeling the need to keep her voice down, "while you continue to check the floors, I'm going to walk along the walls and see if I can find some sort of hidden door that might lead to the lab."

She felt better on her own, and Hudson wasn't giving the impression he really knew what he was looking for.

"All right, cool. Just give me a holler if you find something."

"I will. You do the same."

Samantha broke off from Hudson and headed toward the front of the supply room. She flashed the light from her phone along the drywall, using her hand to push into it in search of a crease or crevice that doubled as a hidden panel.

After several moments of silence, Hudson howled so loudly that Samantha practically jumped out of her boots.

"What's wrong?" she yelped, charging toward the back of the room.

"Woo-hoo!" he wailed.

"Did you find something?"

"I believe I did. Check this out."

Hudson was down on all fours, yanking at a small steel hook that stuck up out of what appeared to be a trap door in the floor.

"Oh wait, there's a padlock securing this thing," he huffed.

Samantha turned to a shelf next to her and dug around inside several boxes until she found a steel pipe.

"Here. Try this."

Hudson grabbed the pipe, raised it high in the air and cracked it against the padlock.

The piercing reverberation of metal on metal caused her to flinch.

"Ooh," she uttered, hunching her shoulders up toward her earlobes as if that would help muffle the clamor. "Did that do it?"

"Not that time. But give me a couple more tries."

After several more attempts at banging the pipe against the lock, Samantha heard pieces of metal skid across the floor.

"You got it?"

"I got it!" he boomed.

She leaned in closer, watching as he grabbed the door's steel loop. He gave it a yank, but the door didn't budge.

"I think it might be stuck," he grunted while continuing to pull at the lever. On the third try, the black panel that blended in perfectly with the floor flew open.

"Yes!" Samantha exclaimed, clapping her hands frantically. She bent down, aiming her cell phone's flashlight into the opening. The minuscule stream of light didn't provide much brightness. All she could make out was what appeared to be a dark abyss.

"Can you see anything down there?" she asked Hudson.

"I'm tryin', but not really." He sat back on his heels and stared off into space. "I cannot friggin' believe this, man. I *told* those dudes on my assembly team that Collin had a secret drug lab hidden somewhere in this place. They just argued me up and down, telling me how wrong I was. *Idiots.*"

"Hudson," Samantha said, eager to get moving, "turn on your cell phone's flashlight so we can get a better look at what's down there."

He sluggishly fumbled around inside his puffy neon-green jacket for several seconds before finally pulling out his phone. After tapping the screen for several seconds, he threw his head back and focused on the ceiling.

"Damn," he wheezed, dumbfounded, his thin, cracked lips hanging open. "What's my security code?"

"You don't need to enter your security code to access the flashlight," Samantha told him, resisting the urge to push him off to the side and make her way down into the opening on her own.

"Got it," he finally said, pressing more buttons until the flashlight came on.

The pair held their lights down into the darkness. A set of extremely steep black stairs appeared. Before she could say a word, Hudson spun around on his knees and began climbing down steps.

"Be careful," she told him.

"I will. But I'm hardheaded. So if I fall, I'll pop right up and keep it moving!" he snorted before emitting an animalistic cackle.

Just get in, get your photos and get out, Samantha told herself.

While he slowly made his way down, she composed a quick text message to Gregory letting him know they'd found what looked to be the drug lab.

There's a trap door in the floor of the supply room, she quickly typed. We're heading down now. More soon!

Samantha sent the message, then carefully began descending the stairs behind Hudson.

"Do you see a light down there anywhere?" she called out.

"I think I see one hanging from the ceiling. I'm trying to find a pull string, or maybe there's a switch somewhere."

As she waited for him to locate the light, Samantha stood in the middle of the stairway and aimed her phone's flashlight around the small, filthy room.

She zoned in on two steel tables covered in blenders, scales, glass cookware and pill bottles. When she climbed down a couple more steps to get a better look, a putrid mixture of toxic chemicals and urine invaded her nostrils.

"I *knew* it," she said to herself, using her free hand to shield her nose. "I knew Collin was using Westman's to manufacture drugs. And look at what we've found here..."

"We just hit the jackpot, man!" Hudson hollered just as he turned on the light. He glanced around the room while rigorously scratching his face.

Samantha watched as Hudson threw his arms out at his sides and spun around like a kid in a candy shop. She resisted the urge to tell him to calm down and instead focused on sending Gregory an update.

Jackpot! she typed, her fingertips flying over the keypad. The drug lab! About to get pix now...

Before she could pull up her phone's camera app, Gregory's response popped up on the screen.

Get what you need then get out ASAP!

Will do.

Samantha closed his message, her hands trembling as she began taking photos of the lab. She zoomed in on the tabletops, large jugs filled with murky liquid and buckets underneath the tables.

Just when Samantha began filming a video, she noticed Hudson shoving several bottles of pills inside his coat pockets.

"Hey, what are you doing?" she asked.

Hudson didn't look up from the table as he continued grabbing every pill bottle in sight.

"What does it look like I'm doing? I'm trying to score some of Collin's TKO for free. Don't trip on it, though. He owes me."

"Isn't TKO the same stuff that put you in the hospital?"

"Whatever…" Hudson panted, sweating profusely while feverishly stuffing as much product inside his pockets as he could. "That was probably just a bad batch."

"What a shame," Samantha muttered underneath her breath.

"Ooh, I'm gonna film a live chat with my boys so they can see all this!" Hudson announced.

"Hudson! *No.* That is not a good idea. We need to keep this place under wraps and focus on getting all the evidence turned in to the authorities. Your boys do not need to know about it."

"Aw, come on, man! Let me have a little fun here."

Samantha's eyes squinted warily at him. "I thought you brought me here to help get justice for Jacob and the rest of the Westman's workers. Not steal a bunch of deadly drugs and video chat with your boys for clout. Come on. Get it together. Don't lose focus on what we're trying to accomplish here."

"All right, fine," Hudson mumbled.

He reluctantly slipped his phone in his back pocket. But as Samantha continued filming her video of the lab, she noticed Hudson lurking around one of the tables and slipping more drugs inside his pockets.

Just let it go and get the rest of your footage, she told herself.

Samantha walked farther into the lab and began taking close-up shots of several propane fuel cylinders. A text message notification from Gregory popped up on the screen. She tapped on it.

You have got to get out of there NOW! it read. Collin and his boys just entered the factory!

Samantha's stomach dropped down to her knees. "Hudson!" she shrieked. "We've gotta go. Collin and his boys just pulled up!"

"Ha-ha, nice joke. They couldn't be here. Him and his crew are hanging out down at the strip club tonight."

"Well, obviously they had a change of plans," Samantha insisted, struggling to make her way up the steep set of stairs. "Detective…a friend…just texted me saying he saw them coming in. Now let's get the hell out of here before we get busted!"

Hudson casually strutted over to a metal cabinet, his filthy white sneakers screeching loudly across the floor.

"Hey!" Samantha hissed as she watched him rummage through the shelves. "This is not a drill. Let's go!"

"Yeah, yeah, I'll be up in a sec."

She couldn't wait. She climbed the stairs, hoping he'd follow. When Samantha reached the top, she froze at the sound of muffled voices coming from beyond the supply room.

"Nah, dude!" someone yelled. "The strippers can wait. They won't care about us being late once I show up with a few bags of that TKO!"

She immediately recognized that sinister voice. Collin.

Samantha spun around and frantically waved her hand in Hudson's direction. But he was buried too deep inside the cabinet to notice.

"They already know what's up!" Collin said, his voice getting closer. "Big Vick is holding our VIP booth at the club, so we're good. The girls, the bottles…everything will be at our table when we get there."

Just as Samantha pulled herself out of the drug lab, she heard the door to the supply room fly open. Footsteps thumped loudly toward the back of the room.

Oh nooo, she thought as memories of her near misses with Collin came to mind.

"I'll make it quick," Collin said. "Just let me grab the product, then we'll be out."

"Cool, man. Do your thing," Samantha heard one of his cronies reply.

She stayed low and darted toward the back wall, then crouched down in a corner behind a shelf stacked with sheet metal.

"Hey!" Collin yelled. "Who the hell left the door to the lab open?"

Samantha cringed at the rage in his tone, swallowing hard as a lump of nausea crept up her throat.

"Not me," each of his boys quickly replied.

All Samantha could think about was Hudson still being down in the lab and what Collin would do if he found him. She prayed that he'd found a good hiding spot.

"I swear I can't trust you fools to do anything right!" Collin continued to rant. "What if the wrong person would've come up in here and found the lab?"

"There's only a few of us who have access to the supply room, though," someone tried to reason. "Only your boys who are closest to you can even get back here."

"I don't give a damn about that!" Collin hollered. "I've got a couple of assembly team leads who have the door code but don't know about the lab. I'm telling you man, y'all better wake up. Don't make me have to unleash my other side. *Trust* me. You do not wanna meet him."

Samantha squeezed her phone in her quivering hand. As she heard the men climbing down the stairs, she composed a text to Gregory.

Collin and his boys are heading down into the drug lab and Hudson's still down there! I'm hiding in the supply room. Should I make a run for it or stay hidden?

While she waited for the detective to respond, Samantha struggled to hear what was happening down in the lab. Just when her phone buzzed, she heard yelling coming from the lab.

"What in the hell are you doing down here?"

She bent down and pressed her ear to the floor.

"Hudson!" she heard Collin bark. "Were you actually dumb enough to creep inside my factory and break into my lab? Wait! Are those my drugs falling out of your pockets? So you're stealing from me, too?"

Samantha swallowed hard. She checked the phone for Gregory's reply.

Stay put! Do not try to run. Don't risk being seen.

The thought of having to stay inside the factory made her shudder. But she knew Gregory was right.

Okay, she wrote back. Collin and his boys are in the lab. They found Hudson.

As soon as Samantha hit the send button, she heard more yelling coming from the lab.

"No, no, *no*! Please, Collin, don't!" Hudson pleaded.

"I am not the one to be messed with," she heard Collin shout. "I can't believe you had the audacity to try me. But hear me when I tell you that you'll never get the chance to do it again."

Samantha clenched her hands together and pressed them against her lips.

"Please, please don't hurt him," she whispered just as Collin yelled, "Hand me that pipe!"

"Come on, man," Hudson begged. "I promise you it'll never happen—"

He was silenced by the brutal sound of a bone cracking.

Hudson emitted an animalistic howl. Samantha covered her mouth, stifling the scream that almost flew out.

"Why'd you do that, man!" she heard Hudson shout. His words were garbled by pain.

"You know why I did it!" Collin yelled. "And you know why I'm about to do this, too."

The sound of another cracking bone numbed Samantha's eardrums. She shook so hard she could barely hold her phone.

"Get him outta here," Collin commanded.

Samantha scrambled to her feet and repositioned herself farther behind the stack of metal. Jumbled voices echoed up the stairs, followed by heavy, stuttering footsteps. Had Hudson given her up? Or had he been too addled to even remember she was here?

She crossed her arms in front of her tightly, shivering uncontrollably at the thought of being found.

When her cell phone began vibrating like crazy, Samantha silenced it completely then opened a string of text messages from Gregory.

What is all that noise? I'm at the door and coming in!

No! she quickly replied. Don't! Collin and his boys are on their way out. They just beat Hudson up!

Samantha sent the text, then braced herself as gurgling moans rippling through the supply room.

"Why didn't you just kill him?" one of Collin's cronies asked.

"Where's the fun in that?" Collin snarked. "I like to teach lessons. And you have to be alive to learn them. Hudson needs to know that Collin Wentworth is never, *ever* to be crossed. These broken bones will be a nice little reminder of that."

"So does this mean you're gonna just keep torturing him instead?" another one of the guys chuckled.

Samantha grimaced at the sound of amusement in his deep, gravelly voice.

"I might," Collin replied. "But I definitely wanna keep him around. Hudson's a good little lab rat. Let's me test out any drug on him that I want before putting it out on the street. Now grab him and let's get out of here."

Just as Samantha heard the men dragging a whimpering Hudson out of the room, her cell phone rang loudly. She stared down at it in horror.

Instead of silencing it, she'd accidentally turned the volume up full blast.

"Whose phone is that?" Collin asked.

A surge of fear detonated inside Samantha's chest. She shook uncontrollably while grappling with the button that turned off the ringer.

Her heart palpitated erratically as she leaned to the side and peered out at the men through a crack in between the shelves.

Hudson was sprawled out on the floor and appeared to be unconscious. Two of Collin's flunkies were standing on either side of him, holding his arms.

"It wasn't my cell," both of them muttered, shrugging while looking around the room.

"Did one of you fools leave your phone down in the lab, or is somebody else in here with us?" Collin spewed, his voice rising with each word.

Samantha held her breath. She froze.

The sound of shuffling feet filled the air. Collin's boys had dropped Hudson's arms and were scrambling around the room.

"So you weren't in here alone, were you, ole Huddy boy?" Collin asked, kicking him savagely in the leg. "And you didn't even bother to *tell* me?"

Samantha curled up into a tight ball, every muscle in her body tense as she braced herself to face Collin's wrath. Her jaws clenched together tightly when she heard Hudson emit a heart-wrenching growl.

"It…it was my—my ph-phone," he sputtered.

"It was your *what*?" Collin yelled, ruthlessly kicking him again.

"It was my phone," Hudson repeated before coughing and gagging. A clump of blood gushed from his mouth.

Samantha pressed her teeth into her fist while she waited for Collin to respond. His boys stopped in their tracks one shelving unit away from where she was hiding.

"Dumbass," Collin muttered. He held his arm in the air, signaling for his boys to come back. "Hey! Let's get the hell out of here. Mitch, text Big Vick and tell him we're running late, but we'll be at the club after we make a quick stop. I need to figure out where to dump this pile of garbage," he spat before nudging Hudson's shoulder with the pipe.

Thank you, thank you, thank you, Samantha thought, beyond grateful that Hudson had looked out for her but still worried for him.

She glanced down at her phone and saw that Gregory had sent her about ten text messages in a row. She opened the most recent one.

If I don't hear from you within the next minute, I'm coming in!

Her fingertips raced across the screen as she responded to the message.

No! Don't!

Send.

They're coming out now!

Send.

And Hudson's still alive.

Send.

I'll be out as soon as they're gone. Stay low and meet me by the door where I came in. Is the guard still out there?

Samantha sent the last message then peered through the shelves. Hudson's feet had gotten caught in the doorway. One of Collin's cronies kicked the door open and yanked the rest of his body out of the room.

She quickly checked her phone for Gregory's reply.

Collin sent the guard to lunch when he got here. I see everybody coming out now. Start making your way to the door. I'll let you know when the coast it clear.

On my way! Samantha typed, both shocked and relieved that she was making it out of the factory alive.

When she stood up, her wobbly legs almost caused her to crash to the floor. She gripped a stack of boxes behind her and steadied her gait, then hurried through the supply room.

She peeked through the door before stepping out. The factory was empty. They didn't have round-the-clock shifts. Just as she crept past several workstations, her cell phone lit up with another text from Gregory.

It's clear. They just pulled off. I'm at the side door. Meet me there now!

Samantha couldn't get to the door fast enough. She darted past a row of equipment assembly systems and crashed through the exit so forcefully that she almost stumbled to the ground. Gregory was standing on the other side. He immediately grabbed hold of her.

"It's okay," he said, lifting her up and embracing her tightly. "Come on. I got you."

Samantha finally allowed herself to breathe. She closed her eyes and leaned into the detective, her feet barely touching the ground as he led them to the car.

"Thank you," she whispered into his chest.

"I'm just glad you're okay."

When he planted a soft kiss on her forehead, Samantha wrapped her arms around him and gripped the back of his jacket.

"I swear I didn't think I'd make it out of there alive."

"Well, you did. And from this point on, I'm never gonna allow you to get in harm's way again. Never. Now let's get out of here."

Gregory held Samantha in a grip so tight she had no doubt he'd keep her safe forever.

Chapter Sixteen

Gregory's heart rate didn't stabilize until he and Samantha were back inside the car and pulling away from Westman's.

He glanced over at her. Her creased brow and downturned lips gave away her shock and fear. She must have been petrified in that factory, yet she'd stuck with it, all to get justice for Jacob and the rest of the factory workers.

When he reached over and covered her hand with his, she jumped a little and gasped.

"Are you okay?" Gregory asked her.

"I was just thinking," she panted, "I bet you could probably catch up with Collin and his boys to see where they're taking Hudson. Maybe I can even try and get some pictures of Hudson's injuries. *Man*, I wish I'd thought of that while we were still inside the factory. But I was so terrified, and—"

"Samantha," Gregory snapped, interrupting her rant. "Please. Stop it. I can't believe that's where your head's at after what just happened. I don't want you going anywhere near Collin again. I mean, seriously, haven't you had enough? What you went through tonight was absolutely horrifying."

She threw her hands in the air in exasperation. "But we need to help Hudson! He helped us! We've come too far to let up now. We've got Collin right where we want him. If we have proof of the drug lab *and* evidence that he brutally assaulted Hudson, there's no way he wouldn't be thrown in jail immediately!"

Gregory bit down on his jaw, struggling to choose his words wisely so not to further upset Samantha.

"We will help Hudson. I will call it in—that we saw someone being beaten and dragged from the factory. I'll reach out to officers I can trust. But you've already put your life on the line not once, but twice trying to collect evidence against Collin. That's done."

Samantha turned toward the window and covered her eyes.

"So that's it?" she asked. "You're not gonna go after him yourself? You're supposed to be serving and protecting the community. Or have you forgotten your job description?"

"Says the woman who broken into Collin's house *and* Westman's Automotive Factory," he shot back. "If I was one hundred percent perfect at serving and protecting the community, you'd be sitting behind bars right about now." He pulled out his phone and was about to dial when Samantha grabbed his arm and pointed up the road.

She leaned forward and squinted her eyes, struggling to get a better look.

"Gregory," she breathed, pointing at the writhing figure, "I think I see a body lying over by the curb."

"What the…" He turned on the engine and drove to where she'd indicated, and the pair jumped out and ran over to the body.

"Hudson!" Samantha screamed when she realized it was him. "Are you okay?"

"Nooo," he wheezed feebly while gripping his chest. "My ribs…my leg…"

"Just hold on," Gregory told him. "We're gonna get you to the hospital—" He brought up his phone, still in his hand.

"No!" Hudson yelled before moaning loudly and doubling over in pain. "Don't take me to the hospital. I don't want anybody to see me like this. Then they'll start asking a bunch of questions, and…"

As his voice trailed off, Samantha gently touched his shoulder. "Hudson, you are severely injured. You need to see a doctor."

"My sister's a nurse. I'll have her come check me out," he grunted through clenched teeth.

"I don't think that's a good idea, Hud—"

"Samantha, *please,*" he whined. "I'm in too much pain to go back and forth with you. Just take me home."

She turned to Gregory, who glanced over at her. After several seconds, he sighed in apparent defeat. "What's your address, Hudson?"

"Wait, so you're just going to take him home?" Samantha whispered. "He's in such bad shape!"

"Do I have a choice? The man made it clear that he doesn't want to go to the hospital and will refuse medical treatment."

"Fifteen thirty-one East Oak Street," Hudson gasped before slumping down.

The detective looked over at Samantha and nodded his head. "Let's get him inside the car."

She carefully lifted Hudson up by the shoulders while Gregory slid his arms underneath his legs. Hudson emitted an agonizing cry as the twosome struggled to slide him inside the back seat.

"I think Collin cracked a few of my ribs," Hudson groaned after Gregory and Samantha jumped inside the car. "And my right leg feels like it might be broken."

"Just hang on," Gregory told him. Once the man was situated, Gregory and Samantha got inside the car, and he gripped the steering wheel as he peeled away from the curb.

As Gregory pressed down on the accelerator, Samantha twisted her lips in frustration.

"After all this," she said to him, "I really hope you'll be contacting the district attorney first thing in the morning. We definitely have enough evidence for him to file charges against Collin and his cohorts now."

The detective remained silent, staring out the window in deep thought as he continued to Hudson's house.

GREGORY STOPPED AT a red light after he and Samantha dropped Hudson off safely at his home. They'd stayed just long enough to make sure the sister arrived to take care of him, and then were on their way.

The detective turned to her, his tired eyes filled with concern. "I didn't want to discuss the situation with the district attorney in front of Hudson. But listen, if I take this new evidence to him, Collin could easily claim that he acted in self-defense after Hudson broke into the factory."

He paused, waiting for Samantha to argue against his point. When she didn't, he went on.

"And," he continued, "I can assure you that Hudson won't report the assault, because he's an addict who knows he was in the wrong tonight. It actually seems as if he feels somewhat beholden to Collin."

When Samantha slowly nodded her head in agreement, Gregory leaned back in his seat. His tense muscles relaxed after realizing that he was finally getting through to her.

"Yeah," she began, "I can see Collin and his boys coming up with any sort of story they want. They could claim that Hudson broke into the factory to steal auto parts, had a weapon, tried to attack them, anything…"

"Exactly. And of course Hudson would be too afraid to tell the truth and report the drug lab."

"Especially considering Collin caught him stealing drugs from it. Speaking of which…"

When the detective stopped at another red light, Samantha pulled out her phone and showed him the photos she'd taken of the lab.

Gregory let out a sharp breath. "He's running a full-blown operation in there."

"Yes, he is. I'll show you the video I filmed when we get back to your place."

Gregory noticed the dejected tone in Samantha's voice. He reached over and gently clutched her hand.

"Hey," he murmured, "come on. Don't get discouraged. You're almost at the finish line. *We're* almost at the finish line. Even though tonight got out of control, you accomplished your mission. But I think that from this point forward, we have to lie low and move smart."

"I know. I'm just ready for all this to be over with," she sighed, wiping away fresh tears. "I want Collin off the street. That man is way more dangerous than I thought. I wish we could just bypass the district attorney altogether and take this case straight to Mayor Elliot."

"Well, keep in mind that when we take Collin down, Chief Wentworth is going down with him. And I'm sure several other law enforcement officers are entangled in their web of illegal dealings, too. According to the DA, he's already informed Mayor Elliot of the case since the chief of police is involved. So that's a good thing. But we still need to make sure the evidence we present was obtained in a legitimate manner, or else every criminal involved could get off on a technicality."

Samantha sighed and threw her head back against the headrest. "I understand. I just hate having to stay silent, knowing what's really going on. I can't even use my blog to vent my frustrations because you've forced me to go dark for the time being."

"I *advised* you to go dark," he argued, steering the car down his block. "Not forced. I can't force you to do anything, Miss Independent. Let's take tonight, for example…"

Samantha stared down at her hands while fidgeting with her fingernails. The minute Gregory pulled into his driveway, she hopped out of the car and sauntered toward the house. He quickly climbed out and followed her to the door.

"Look," he said, "you and I are conducting an intricate, complicated investigation here. This is going to take time."

"I know. Can we just go inside now? I need a drink."

The detective stared down at her. She kept her eyes on the ground. The corners of her mouth were curled into a frown. It was clear that she was hurting. She was just as frustrated as he was, and he knew she understood that everything she'd collected would have to be verified or collected again with warrants and more.

"Hey, come here," he whispered, instinctively taking her in his arms and embracing her tenderly. He reveled in the feeling of her hands gliding across his shoulders, then clenching behind his neck.

After several moments, Gregory's palms slid down Samantha's back and rested on her hips. He pulled away and took her chin in his hand, raising her head until she looked him in the eyes.

"Why don't we pull the plug on this conversation for now?" he suggested. "Let's go inside, and I'll light up the fireplace then pour you that drink. How does that sound?"

"That sounds good."

As the pair entered the house, Gregory hoped that Samantha would be able to relax while he took some time to think. He knew they needed to wrap this case up soon before she took another risk to get it done herself.

The danger and threats were at an all-time high. Gregory had come too close to losing Samantha tonight. He couldn't let it happen again.

Chapter Seventeen

The next morning, Samantha couldn't stop herself from pacing the living room floor. Gregory had just left for work, and her mind was still racing from yesterday's events.

She'd tossed and turned all night. Conjured-up images of Hudson lying on the factory floor after being beaten by Collin flooded her mind. The agony on his crumpled face as he writhed in pain haunted her dreams during the few moments that she was able to fall asleep.

"Stop it," Samantha told herself, shaking her head rapidly as if that would push the thoughts out of her mind. She trudged over to the kitchen counter and grabbed her cell phone.

Don't do it...

She sighed deeply and put the phone back down, then once again paced the floor. A restless anxiety rushed through her limbs, making it impossible to sit still. She wondered what time Gregory planned on doing a discreet drive-by past Hudson's house, which he'd promised he would do at some point during the day to try and check on him. She'd attempted to convince him to let her ride along, but the detective flat out refused.

"Are you serious?" he'd asked. "What if someone

saw us together? That could ruin everything we've been working toward, not to mention put us both in serious danger."

Samantha had to admit that Gregory was right. But now here she was, alone in the house and eager to keep moving forward on the investigation, all while feeling forced to take a step back.

She shuffled into the kitchen and poured herself a second cup of coffee, then took a seat at the dining room table. Samantha realized she had to do something to get her mind off Hudson, Collin and last night's catastrophe. So she opened her laptop and began editing her most recent article for the women's journal.

After giving it one last read, she emailed the piece to her editor. When she closed her inbox, *Someone Knows Something*'s home page popped up on the screen.

Samantha hadn't posted any updates on Jacob's murder in days. Her fingertips were itching to type. She missed the blog. The fact that she hadn't been able to keep the community updated on her investigation and interact with readers left Samantha feeling empty and disconnected. But as Gregory insisted time and time again, continuing to cover the case wasn't worth risking her life.

Her eyes wandered down to the lower right-hand corner of the screen. There were twenty-four unread messages in her blog's inbox.

Do not open them. Do not open them, she kept telling herself.

Reader questions or comments could easily trigger her need to investigate more, and Gregory had been right to caution her about getting evidence legally. But she was dying to know what the townspeople were say-ing about Jacob's case. Maybe there was a lead here.

She squinted her eyes, tapping her fingernails on the keyboard while staring at the screen. Temptation forced her to slide the cursor toward the message in-box. Just as it hovered over the unopened envelope, her cell phone rang.

The shrill ringtone practically jolted her out of her chair. She glanced down at the caller ID, hoping it was Gregory. But no name appeared on the screen. The call registered as unknown.

Oh no...

A weight of panic dropped into the pit of her stom-ach. She grappled with whether or not she should an-swer the call. Maybe it was just spam, a telemarketer. By the time she decided to grab it, the call went to voice mail.

Just as she set it back down, the phone rang again.

"Yep, this is not good..." she muttered, bracing her-self before finally hitting the accept button on the third ring.

"Hello?" she uttered into the phone, struggling not to sound as timid as she felt.

"Hey, Sam! It's Ava."

"Oh, thank goodness!" Samantha breathed. "You have no idea how happy I am to hear your voice. I thought it may have been—"

"Wait," Ava interrupted, "let me guess. You thought it might be Collin?"

"Yes. How did you know?"

"The security guard who was working at Westman's last night called and told me some of what went down.

He knows I'm trying to find out what happened with Jacob and keeps in touch."

"Girl," Samantha practically choked, "it was unreal!"

"Wait," Ava interjected, "before you get into that, I've got some good news to share with you."

"Well, I could certainly use some good news right about now. What's up?"

"Kenzie is alive and well."

Samantha jumped up from her chair as tears of joy immediately filled her eyes. "Is she? I am so happy to hear that! How'd you find out?"

"Her boyfriend, Alex, called me early this morning and told me that she reached out to him last night."

"Really," Samantha said, now pacing the floor. "So, where is she? And why'd she just up and vanish like that?"

"She's hiding out in Alabama at her great-aunt's house. Long story short, she was terrified after Jacob and the other Westman's workers were killed and afraid she'd be next."

"Well, that's perfectly understandable. But wait, what about the email she'd allegedly sent to Alex that ended up coming from an IP address belonging to Collin?"

"Good question. According to Alex, Kenzie sent the message from one of the computers located in Westman's break room. So even though it came through Collin's IP address, she was in fact the one who wrote it."

"Wow," Samantha breathed, walking over to the window and peeking outside. "I can't say I much blame her for abruptly skipping town like that considering all the madness surrounding the factory. I'm just glad to hear she's okay. But wait, speaking of madness, did the security guard at Westman's tell you that Collin beat up Hudson? *Really* badly?"

"Wait, *what*? No! He did tell me that Hudson had somehow gotten injured when he saw Collin and his boys drag him out of the factory. But I don't think he realized that Hudson had been beaten."

"Well, he was," Samantha confirmed, "with a steel pipe, no less."

"I cannot believe this," Ava choked. "I've been trying to get ahold of Hudson to see if he's okay. But the calls have been going straight to voice mail, and he hasn't responded to any of my text messages."

Samantha walked back over to the dining room table and slumped down in her chair. "I am so worried about him. He was bludgeoned pretty badly. And Collin just hauled him out of the factory then tossed him onto the street a few blocks away from Westman's like a bag of trash."

"That man is so disgusting."

"He really is. Luckily Gregory and I spotted Hudson and picked him up. But he refused to go to the hospital and insisted we take him home."

"Unreal…" Ava sighed, pausing briefly before continuing. "Wait, weren't you inside the factory with Hudson?"

Samantha hopped up out of her chair and began pacing the floor again. "I was. And being in there while Hudson was assaulted was an absolute nightmare."

"But how is it that Collin caught him and not you, too?"

Samantha cringed as the memory of Hudson refusing to leave the drug lab popped into her head. "I warned Hudson when I heard Collin and his boys walking through the factory and told him we needed to get out of there. But he was too busy stealing drugs to listen to me—"

"Hold on," Ava interjected. "What do you mean, he was stealing drugs?"

"Oh girl, we've got a lot to catch up on. Hudson and I found an underground drug lab inside the factory. And despite Hudson having gone through Westman's drug rehabilitation program, he's clearly still an addict. Because he was in there trying to snatch up every bottle of dope he could find."

"Wow. And here I was, thinking he was clean."

"Not at all," Samantha continued. "I got out of the lab in time, but wasn't able to leave the factory before Collin and his boys came in. So I was hiding behind a shelf in the supply room when they discovered Hudson. And bless Hudson's heart, he saved me by not telling them I was there."

"This entire situation just keeps getting worse and worse."

"It really does."

"So what now?" Ava asked. "Is Detective Harris *finally* going to turn in all this evidence you two have gathered so that Collin and his boys can be arrested?"

"He will. Eventually…"

"What do you mean, *eventually*?"

"Ava, there is so much more to this story than you know. Things aren't as cut-and-dried as they may seem. Just know that Gregory is doing all that he can to get justice for Jacob and the other Westman's workers. It's only a matter of time."

When Ava grew silent, Samantha became nervous, thinking that she'd hit a nerve.

"Are you still there?" she asked her.

After a few moments, Ava spoke up.

"Yep, I'm here. I'm just trying to figure out when enough is going to be enough. How many more people need to suffer at Collin's hands before he gets locked up?"

The question left Samantha speechless. Because deep down, she felt the exact same way. But ultimately, her loyalty remained with Detective Harris, and she had to trust his process.

"You know what we should do?" Ava continued. "You and I should go by Hudson's house and check on him. What do you think?"

Samantha's eyes widened at the suggestion. She took a long, contemplative sip of coffee.

"Ava, please don't tempt me."

"Come on. I'm serious. This is all getting out of hand. I want to make sure Hudson's okay. In an extremely discreet way, of course."

"You know, before Gregory left for work this morning, he did say that he'd take a drive past Hudson's house to check on him. It probably wouldn't be a good idea for you and me to go by there, considering Collin and his boys may be watching the place. So, as much as I'd love to go with you, I'm going to have to pass. I promised Gregory I'd stay out of trouble."

"You? Stay out of trouble? Since when?"

"Since that disastrous confrontation at Westman's last night."

"Humph. All right then. Suit yourself."

"And Ava? I'd strongly suggest you stay away from Hudson's house as well. It's just too dangerous. Let's leave it to a professional and see what Gregory comes back with."

"So you don't want to check on Hudson with me, even though he's the one who led you to the drug lab?"

"I can't, Ava. I'm sorry."

"So that's it? Have you suddenly forgotten that we set out on this journey to get justice for Jacob *together*? That was your promise to my family and me. But now that you've linked up with Detective Harris, you suddenly wanna start separating yourself from me?"

A streak of guilt burned Samantha's throat. She opened her mouth to speak, but nothing came out but a breath of hollow air.

"And just think, I actually believed we were friends."

"We are friends. I just… It's just that—"

"No, no," Ava interrupted. "You don't have to explain yourself. I've already heard enough. And on that note, I'd better let you go. I don't want to end up saying something that I'll regret later."

"I hate that this is where we are right now. But just hang tight. I promise you, Gregory and I will be making some major moves soon. Trust me on this."

Samantha waited to hear Ava's response, but she said nothing.

"Can you at least promise me you won't go to Hudson's house?"

"I don't know…"

"Listen. I'll send Gregory a text message right now and find out what time he's planning on going by there. As soon as I hear back, I'll let you know. Okay?"

"Fine. But just know that my family and I are running out of patience, and you and Detective Harris are running out of time. If you two don't make something happen soon, then the Jennings family will take matters into our own hands. And trust me, you do not want that problem."

Ava's ominous words sent a chill through Samantha. Before she could respond, Ava continued.

"I'll be looking out for your message once you hear back from Detective Harris. I just hope Hudson's okay."

"So do I. I'll circle back with you soon."

Samantha disconnected the call. An uneasy feeling stirred in the pit of her stomach as she composed a text message to Gregory.

Hey, just got off the phone with Ava. She knows about Hudson and what went down at Westman's last night. She's extremely angry, and the Jennings family is getting impatient. What time are you planning on driving by Hudson's? Ava's really worried about him and I'd love to give her an update before she does something rash...

Samantha sent the message, then glanced over at her computer. A new notification had popped up on her blog. Temptation won out.

She clicked on the comment. When it appeared, she immediately regretted her decision.

Stop digging, bitch, or you'll be digging your own grave next...

GREGORY SAT AT his desk, combing through Jacob's case file. He'd studied it time and time again. But he was giving it yet another look, just to make sure he hadn't missed anything.

At this point, the detective could literally recite every word in the report verbatim. Once he reached the last page, he realized that there wasn't a thing he'd overlooked. He'd hoped to find something he could hang a search warrant on.

He sighed deeply before closing the file. In spite of his coffee being cold, he drained the cup, hoping the last few sips of caffeine would help give him a boost. After last night's madness at Westman's, he'd barely slept and had been dragging all morning.

He refreshed his email inbox. There were no new messages. He'd been planning on driving by Hudson's house to check on him during his lunch break. But since things were quiet around the station, he decided to take advantage of the downtime and go now.

Gregory grabbed Jacob's file. After shoving his keys and cell phone inside his pocket, he walked out of his office.

On the way to the exit, he was surprised to hear Chief Wentworth call out his name.

"Hey, Detective Harris, can I see you in my office?"

Gregory stopped abruptly. He looked through the chief's doorway and saw him sitting behind the desk, one of his hefty arms propped up on his elbows as he thumbed through a report.

"Of course."

"Close the door behind you."

Gregory stepped inside the office apprehensively and closed the door. He eyed the chief, searching the blank expression on his chubby face for some sort of indication as to why he'd called him in.

"Have a seat," Chief Wentworth told him.

Just as he grabbed hold of a chair, Gregory's cell

phone buzzed. He pulled it from his pocket and saw a text message from Samantha appear on the screen. He slipped it back inside his pocket and sat down.

"The reason I called you in here is because I wanted to let you know I hadn't forgotten about the police reports that were filed on Samantha Vincent."

"Oh..." the detective muttered, the tension in his shoulders easing up at the sound of those words. "That's good to hear."

"Just know that the investigations are still active. I'm really trying to get to the bottom of who was behind those attacks on her house. I'm not coming up with much, since there were no eyewitnesses. And the DNA tests came back inconclusive on the evidence you submitted on that first report. Well, with the exception of Officer Baxter's fingerprints, which showed up on one of the bricks you collected."

"Of course," Gregory quipped.

"Speaking of Officer Baxter, I enrolled him and Officer Miller in a crime scene investigation refresher course. Like you'd said, their inspection of Miss Vincent's home and subsequent reporting was shoddy to say the least."

Gregory stared across the cluttered desk at Chief Wentworth, momentarily at a loss for words. He watched the chief run his hands over the silver-gray stubble lining his plump jowls.

"I, uh...*wow*," the detective said. "Thanks, Chief. I have to admit, I hadn't expected anything to come out of that."

"Yeah, well, there's been a lot happening around here. My main focus has been on the department's budget that Mayor Elliot and I are working to finalize. So some of my other priorities have fallen by the wayside. But I'm back on top of things."

Detective Harris watched the chief closely as he casually reclined in his chair and scratched at his sparse crew cut. Knowing he was involved in his son's deadly drug ring was hard to swallow.

"That's good to know," Gregory replied, maintaining a poker face that rivaled the chief's. "I guess I just assumed you'd forgotten about the investigations."

"Never assume, Detective. You know what that makes us both," he chuckled.

Before Gregory could respond, Chief Wentworth's phone rang. He held up a finger, gesturing for the detective to excuse him, then picked up one of two cell phones that was sitting near his landline.

"Chief Wentworth," he barked, his thick eyebrows furrowing deeply into his wrinkled forehead. "Hey, Larry. Yeah, I've been waiting on your call. What have you got for me?"

The chief swiveled back and forth in his worn, squeaky leather chair. His mouth hung open as he listened keenly to the voice on the other end of the call.

Gregory studied the contents on his desk. Stacks of papers surrounded Chief Wentworth's computer monitor and laptop. A few disposable cups were scattered in between the piles. There was a file hanging off the side of the desk underneath a black letter tray. The detective focused on the name scrawled across the tab, which read Axel Guzman.

Detective Harris's eyes blinked rapidly as he racked his brain trying to recollect where he'd heard the name. And then it dawned on him. Axel Guzman was a major drug dealer connected to a notorious Midwest drug cartel that he'd become familiar with while working in Chicago.

Gregory's heart pounded out of his chest. His mind churned in a thousand different directions. If Axel was involved in Collin and Chief Wentworth's drug ring, that meant he and Samantha were no longer just investigating a little drug lab located in the basement of Westman's Automotive Factory. They were entangled in a full-blown mafia-level operation.

"So you got him?" Chief Wentworth said into the phone. "Are you *sure* you got him?"

The chief turned his back to Gregory and stared up at the certificates hanging on the wall. The detective focused on him while scooting toward the edge of his chair. He slid Axel's file off the desk and tucked it in between the reports in his hand.

"All right then, Larry," Chief Wentworth continued. "Good work, per usual. I appreciate you. Yeah, I'll shoot you the payment the usual way. No problem. Yep. Thanks for the great work. Oh, you know I'll be needing you again, sooner rather than later, I'm sure. Okay, I'll be in touch."

He disconnected the call and tossed his phone onto the desk. "Sorry about that, Detective. Just had a little business that I needed to take care of."

"No problem," Gregory replied, anxious to get out of the station and pore over Axel's file with Samantha.

"So that's all I've got for you," the chief continued. "Got anything for me?"

He sat for a few moments, as if thinking of something he needed to report. "No, I think I covered everything at our last update meeting."

"Okay, then." Chief Wentworth glanced down at his

watch. "I need to get out of here. I've got a luncheon down at city hall that I need to get to. Everything else going okay for you? I hope Gattenburg's not moving too slow for you compared to all that action you had going on back in the Windy City."

"No, not at all. Everything's going great for me here in Gattenburg. I'm actually enjoying the slower pace." Gregory paused, studying the chief closely before continuing. "You know, one thing I had been concerned with was those Westman's workers whose bodies were recovered in Galena. While their fate was unfortunate, I'm glad their cold cases were finally solved and the families received closure."

"Yeah," the chief sighed, staring solemnly at Gregory. "That was definitely a tragic situation. My son, Collin, implemented an excellent rehabilitation program for recovering addicts at Westman's. Sadly, it doesn't always work for everyone. My heart goes out to those young men who overdosed as well as their families. Like you, I'm glad their cases were solved."

Gregory stared back at his boss, shocked by what appeared to be a genuine show of sympathy.

Chief Wentworth stood up and tugged at his snug navy slacks. "*Whoa*, I guess it's time for me to start that low-carb diet my wife's been nagging me about. But anyway, why don't you and I circle back later this week? I feel like I haven't been giving you enough face time since you've joined the force."

Gregory was slow to respond. He stood up and followed the chief out of the office. The detective couldn't help but wonder whether his boss was trying to get closer to him because he was on to his and Samantha's investigation.

"That would be great, thanks," Gregory told him despite feeling otherwise. He clutched the files in his hand even tighter, eager to get out of the station.

Chief Wentworth stopped at the front desk. Gregory quickly brushed past him and jetted out the door.

He walked through the parking lot and inhaled the crisp air, relieved to finally be away from the chief.

On the way to his car, Gregory noticed Officers Baxter and Miller hovering near the back of the lot. In between puffing on cigarettes, they simultaneously threw him looks of disgust.

"What's up, guys!" Gregory called out, stifling a laugh as he climbed inside his car. He wasn't surprised when neither of them responded.

The detective sped out of the lot and headed toward Hudson's house. On the way there, he pulled out his cell phone. Five missed calls from Samantha appeared on the screen.

"Oh no," he moaned. "This can't be good…"

He immediately dialed her number. She picked up on the first ring.

"Gregory!" she panted, "where are you?"

"I'm heading to Hudson's house to check on him. Why? What's going on?"

"I've been receiving death threats for the past hour. Phone calls, text messages, comments on my blog. They're all coming in anonymously, but I know it's Collin."

Gregory's jaw tightened. "What is he saying, exactly?"

"That he's going to hunt me down and slit my throat."

"My God…" Gregory floored the gas pedal. "Make

sure all the doors and windows are locked, and just hang tight. I'll be there in a few minutes."

When she didn't respond, he continued.

"Just calm down," the detective told her. "Collin doesn't even know where you are."

"Someone is calling me on the other line."

"*Don't* answer it."

Samantha sat silently on the other end of the phone.

"Are you still there?" Gregory asked.

"I am. I was just checking to see whether a name registered on the caller ID. I think it's Ava. I should take it. She may be getting death threats, too."

"Okay. Go ahead and answer it."

"Hold on."

As she clicked over to the other line, Gregory sped through a yellow light. He'd never been one to scare easily, but in this moment, his entire body burned with fear.

"Gregory!" Samantha whispered into the phone after clicking back over. "Collin is dead!"

"Wait, what?" he asked, convinced that he'd heard her wrong.

"Collin is dead!" she repeated, louder this time. "Ava just told me!"

"How does she know that?" Detective Harris asked skeptically.

"Hudson called and told her. Collin and his boys had stopped by his house to warn him that he'd better keep his mouth shut about the incident at Westman's. When Collin was walking back to his truck, someone drove up and shot him!"

Gregory tore down his block and pulled into the driveway. "I'm here. I'll be inside in a—"

Before he could finish, Samantha threw open the

front door and ran out to the car. The detective jumped out and embraced her tightly. He caressed her back as she sobbed into his chest.

"What is happening right now?" she cried.

"Everything's going to be okay," he whispered.

"No, it isn't, Gregory. Somebody is on a killing spree in this town, and we've been after the wrong person this entire time! Our investigation is back at square one. How is everything going to be okay?"

He pulled away from Samantha and rested his hands on her shoulders. Aching pangs filled his chest at the sight of her wild, terror-filled eyes.

The detective led her inside the house and quickly closed the door behind them.

"We're going to Mayor Elliot's house," he declared. "Tonight."

Samantha turned to him, her entire face lighting up. "Really?"

"Yes. This situation has gotten completely out of hand. At this point I don't know who's out to get whom. I just had a talk with Chief Wentworth before leaving the station, and he seemed perfectly fine. As a matter of fact, I was surprised to hear he's investigating the crimes that were committed against you and took further action against Officers Baxter and Miller."

"I am so confused right now..." Samantha shuffled over to the couch and fell into the cushions. "This entire situation has my head spinning. I wonder if Chief Wentworth knows that Collin's been killed yet."

"Good question." Gregory checked his phone. "I haven't gotten any calls or text messages. But judging from the way these guys roll, they probably wouldn't report the crime. They'd hide Collin's body and seek revenge."

"Judging from the way these guys roll, I wouldn't be surprised if Chief Wentworth had something to do with it."

Detective Harris stared at her, absorbing what she'd just said. He slowly walked over to the couch and took a seat next to her.

"You know, it's funny you say that. When I was in the chief's office, he did have a rather interesting phone conversation that I overheard."

"Did he? With who?"

"Some guy named Larry. The conversation just seemed…odd. Chief Wentworth was saying things like, 'So you got him? Are you sure you got him?' Then he told the guy that he'd done a good job and he would send him his payment."

Gregory glanced over at Samantha and saw that she was staring back at him in shock.

"Are you thinking what I'm thinking?" she whispered.

"That Chief Wentworth put a hit out on his own son?" He had a hard time getting his head wrapped around that.

Samantha nodded her head while she massaged her temples. "Well, if the chief thought Collin was getting too careless in the way he was handling their drug operation, then yes. Absolutely. I've seen firsthand how ruthless these men can be."

Gregory grabbed the files he'd taken from the police station. "And to add to the suspense, I found a report in Chief Wentworth's office on Axel Guzman—"

"Wait, Axel Guzman—where have I heard that name?"

"He's a drug dealer. Part of a big Midwest cartel."

"Oh my God…" Samantha covered her mouth with her hands. "Do you think he's working with Chief Wentworth and Collin?"

"That would be my guess. And you already know how he moves. The man is a savage. If Collin crossed him, he also could've been the one to have him killed."

Samantha was visibly shaken. She ran her hands over her arms, as if trying to warm herself up.

"I want to take this to the mayor, but he's not available until this evening. Let's go check on Hudson, then head there."

They gazed at one another, the energy between them palpable. In that moment, Gregory realized that the imminent danger surrounding them had only brought them even closer together. He wanted this case over so she'd be out of danger and in his arms for more than just protection.

Chapter Eighteen

"I am really not looking forward to telling Mayor Elliot about Chief Wentworth and Collin's drug ring," Gregory muttered to Samantha as they headed to the mayor's house. They'd already done a quick check on Hudson, who was recovering from his injuries.

"I know," Samantha said, gripping the thick file of information that she and Gregory had compiled tightly. "He is going to be crushed. He thinks the world of the chief."

She stared out the window, thoughts of the day's outrageous events flashing through her mind. "I still can't believe Collin is dead."

"Neither can I. But in all honesty, we shouldn't be surprised. Look at all the damage he's done and bridges he's burned all over this town."

"Very true." Samantha turned to the detective, her eyelids lowering with doubt. "But at this point, I'm wondering whether Collin's only guilty of manufacturing illegal drugs and injuring Hudson. What if he isn't the one behind the deaths of Jacob and the other Westman's workers?"

The detective raised his eyebrows curiously. "That's a definite possibility. But at this point, things have gotten way too baffling to assume anything. That's why we're going to Mayor Elliot. Maybe he'll be the one to pull the truth out of Chief Wentworth."

"I hope so."

Gregory turned down the mayor's block and eased up on the accelerator. As he approached the house, all the lights appeared to be out.

"I wonder if he's home," Detective Harris said before pulling up to the curb and parking the car.

"There's only one way to find out." Samantha ignored the jitters flitting throughout her entire body. She closed her eyes, said a quick prayer, then grabbed the door handle. "Come on. Let's do this."

The pair climbed out of the car and approached Mayor Elliot's grand, pillared white porch. Gregory searched the street, checking to see whether anyone was in the vicinity.

"Looks like the coast is clear," he said.

Samantha reached up to ring the doorbell. Right before her finger hit the button, a bloodcurdling shout came from the back of the house.

She jerked her hand away and grabbed the detective's arm. "What the hell was that?"

Gregory reached back and pulled his gun out of his waistband. "Go back to the car. Lock the doors."

"No way."

He muttered a curse and heaved a sigh. "Let's go check around back. Stay behind me."

Samantha didn't release her grip on the detective's arm as he led her along the side of the house. They approached a tall wooden gate. Just as he slowly opened it, another ear-piercing shriek ripped through the air, drowning out the sound of the gate's creaking wood.

"*Help!* Please, somebody help me!"

Gregory turned to Samantha. "Wait, that sounds like Chief Wentworth!"

He led her into the dark, vast backyard. They slunk up the stairs leading to the deck. Samantha held Gregory tighter as they crept alongside the brick wall, then paused at the edge of sliding glass doors. A set of semi-sheer white curtains partially covered them.

"Can you see anything?" she whispered.

Gregory turned to her and held his finger to his lips, signaling her silence. She nodded her head, then cringed at the sound of more yelling.

"Just sign the damn papers, Wentworth!"

"What is going *on* in there?" she mouthed.

Gregory took a slight step to the side and peered through the glass. She peeked past him and peered through the curtain.

"What the…"

In the dim light, she saw Mayor Elliot standing over Chief Wentworth with a knife to his throat. The chief was tied to a chair, his distorted expression twisted in terror.

"Sign them! *Now!*" the mayor shouted as he shoved a stack of papers in the chief's face.

Samantha quickly stepped away from the door. Every one of her limbs trembled as she processed what they were witnessing.

"I'm not signing a damn thing!" Chief Wentworth shot back. "You killed my son, and you think I'm gonna take the blame for it? You're out of your mind!"

"What is happening right now?" Samantha whimpered, shaking her head in utter confusion.

"Your son was a loose cannon, Walter!" the mayor

spewed. "He was getting out of control. Killing the townspeople with his deadly drug experiments. But after he savagely beat Hudson, who just so happens to be the district attorney's stepson? That was the last straw."

Samantha and Gregory turned to one another, gasping in unison after hearing the information about Hudson.

"Collin would never—" Chief Wentworth began. He was abruptly silenced when Mayor Elliot pressed the knife into his throat.

"That's your problem!" the mayor yelled. "You raised your son to be a punk! Thanks to you, he never paid for any of his wrongdoings. And now? He's right where he belongs, and you're going to take the blame for him almost taking my entire drug operation down."

Samantha and Gregory both froze. Mayor Elliot was involved in Gattenburg's drug ring.

When Chief Wentworth cried out in pain, Samantha turned to Gregory.

"You have got to do something! *Now!*"

Without saying a word, the detective used the butt of his gun to break the lock on the door. He threw it open and aimed the weapon at Mayor Elliot.

"Drop the knife!" he yelled.

Chief Wentworth let out a sigh of relief when he laid eyes on Gregory and Samantha. The mayor, however, appeared stunned. But his mouth quickly twisted into a shrewd smirk.

"So how much did you two hear?" he asked condescendingly.

"Enough to know that you're running a drug ring

and killed Collin," Gregory shot back. "Now drop the knife and step away from Chief Wentworth."

"Aww, how sweet," Mayor Elliot said. "Look, everybody, it's the new kid on the block, trying to be a hero. Listen, you and your little fake journalist friend here need to get the hell out of my house. Trust me, you don't wanna get involved in this."

"Don't listen to him," Chief Wentworth pleaded. "Help me. The mayor's trying to force me to sign a statement confessing that I'm involved in his drug operation and responsible for the murders of Jacob and Collin—"

"Shut up!" Mayor Elliot yelled, slicing the chief's jaw with the knife.

"Ahh!" Chief Wentworth hollered in agony. "Shoot him, Harris. *Shoot* him!"

"Drop the weapon, Elliot!" Gregory once again insisted. "I'm not going to ask you again."

Smirking, the mayor tossed the knife across the room. When Gregory turned to retrieve it, Mayor Elliot fled the room.

"Untie him," Gregory yelled to Samantha, nodding toward the chief before running after the mayor.

Samantha swooped in and began tugging at the knots restraining Chief Wentworth.

"Are you okay?" she asked him.

"My boy is dead," the chief whimpered. "He's dead!"

"I'm so sorry," she replied while frantically untying him. "Come on. Let's get you out of here and call for backup."

Samantha bent down and wrapped Chief Wentworth's arm around her shoulders, helping him out of the chair. He leaned into her, his hefty frame causing her to stumble. She swiftly regained her footing and led him out the door toward the front of the house. On the way there, she managed to grab hold of her cell phone and dial 9-1-1, spitting out the information about what was going on and telling the dispatcher she didn't need to stay on the line.

"I can't believe my boy is gone," Wentworth mumbled. He fell against the side of the house, sobbing into the palms of his hands.

Samantha bent down and wrapped her arm around the chief.

"I mean—I knew Collin was trouble," he continued. "But I had no idea he was into all this. It's my fault. I should've disciplined him more. I shouldn't have let him get away with all that I did over the years."

Samantha grabbed a tissue from her coat pocket and held it to the chief's jaw. She couldn't ignore his pain, despite his connection to the harm that'd been done to so many.

"Collin chose this life," Chief Wentworth declared. "But he just didn't have it in him to walk the straight and narrow. I hope you know I had nothing to do with any of this."

"Collin kept a drug ledger that implicated you."

The chief nodded his head solemnly, the corners of his damp eyes crinkling with sadness. "I know. I just found out about all this from Officer Barris. He confided in me while we were down at city hall this afternoon."

"Wait, Officer Barris knew about the drug ring?"

"Yes. He did. He'd just recently found out about it after Officers Baxter and Miller tried to recruit him into Guzman's crime syndicate. Guzman and Mayor

Elliot are behind all this. And they've been paying off several Gattenburg police officers to turn a blind eye and keep quiet."

"I knew those two were somehow involved. That's why they blew off the vandalism investigation at my house. They've been working against my cause to get justice for Jacob Jennings all along."

"Barris also found out that Guzman is the anonymous owner of Westman's Automotive Factory. He registered the ownership under a different name so that it wouldn't be affiliated with him."

"And so he could use it produce illegal drugs," Samantha added. "Without it being traced to him."

"Exactly. Those drugs that Collin was formulating were so potent. And deadly. Some concoction he was trying to perfect called TKO is what killed the three Westman's workers. They were testing it out one night inside the factory. After they OD'd, Guzman ordered *my* son to dump their bodies in the woods somewhere outside Gattenburg. And Collin did it."

He paused, his voice cracking as he began to sob uncontrollably. Samantha wrapped her arm around him, patting his back until he gathered himself.

"And poor Jacob," the chief continued, his distorted words practically inaudible. "He was just trying to find out what happened to his coworkers when he went to talk to Collin. But Collin made the mistake of telling Guzman, who turned around and killed Jacob with a deadly overdose in order to silence him."

Samantha blinked back tears, thinking of how Ava would take the news.

"I'm in shock right now," Chief Wentworth muttered, staring straight ahead as if he were in a daze. "I came here thinking Mayor Elliot would help me apprehend my son's killer. Instead he attacks me, and I find out he's in on the whole operation. He's the one who convinced Collin to list my name in the drug ledger so that if it were ever confiscated, I'd be implicated and forced to cover for them."

"I'm so sorry, Chief. I, um—I actually have Collin's drug ledger in my possession."

"You do? How did you get ahold of it?"

"It's complicated," Samantha said just as she heard yelling come from inside the house.

"Drop the gun, Elliot! *Now!*"

Bang. Bang. Bang.

Samantha inhaled sharply, immobilized by the thought of Gregory being shot.

"Let's go!" Chief Wentworth yelled. He pulled her up and led her toward the street. They crouched down behind Gregory's car.

Samantha stared out at the mayor's house. *Come out, Gregory, please come out.*

"I've gotta get in there!" she insisted, jumping up. "I need to make sure Gregory's okay…"

"Samantha, *no!*" Chief Wentworth grabbed hold of her. "Detective Harris is well trained and knows how to handle himself. You might endanger him if you go in. Help is on the way."

As soon as he spoke those words, sirens blared in the distance. Samantha spun around and saw flashing lights heading their way. She jumped up and waved her arms in the air. Officer Barris was the first one to pull up and jump out of his car.

"Detective Harris is inside the house and Mayor Elliot is trying to kill him!" she yelled.

"Got it!" the officer called out, leading a trail of officers through the front yard. They broke down the door and barreled inside.

She couldn't wait any longer and started rushing toward the door herself.

Before she got far, Gregory came limping through the front door with policemen on either side of him, his left leg covered in blood.

Samantha ran to the detective at full speed.

"Are you okay?" she managed to say, her voice choked.

"I will be," Gregory muttered through clenched teeth. "Mayor Elliot shot me. It just grazed me. Officer Barris stopped the bleeding."

Samantha knew he was downplaying his injury for her sake. As he spoke, she saw him wince in pain.

"We need to get you to the hospital, Detective Harris," Officer Barris told him. "The ambulance is waiting."

"I'm coming with you," Samantha insisted. "There's no way I'm letting you out of my sight."

"I don't want you to…"

As the group headed toward the ambulance, they stopped to check on Chief Wentworth. He was leaning against a squad car now, holding a fresh handkerchief against his wounded jaw.

"Detective Harris," the chief said, "I can't thank you and Samantha enough for what you did tonight. You two saved my life."

"I was just doing my job, sir," Gregory replied. "With the help of the best criminal journalist in town. Samantha was crucial in getting to the bottom of all this."

"Thanks," she whispered, a smile of appreciation spreading across her face.

"Well, you two make a great team," Chief Wentworth said. "Now get out of here. Get to the hospital and have them stitch up that leg."

"Will do, sir. And you have my condolences. I'm really sorry about what happened to Collin."

Chief Wentworth nodded silently, his lips tightening as he blinked back tears. "Hey, before you go, Detective, I have something I want to share with you."

"What's that?"

"After tonight, I'll be retiring. And I'm going to recommend you as my replacement. I had my eye on you for this slot when I hired you."

Gregory stared at Chief Wentworth in disbelief. "Wow. I...I don't know what to say, sir. Thank you."

"You're welcome. It's well deserved. We'll talk more about it later. For now, get to the hospital. And while you're there, start thinking about the capital murder, aggravated kidnapping and drug trafficking charges that need to be brought against Elliot and Guzman."

"Yes, sir."

The group said their goodbyes, and the EMTs came over and helped Gregory inside the ambulance. Samantha climbed in behind him and took a seat next to the stretcher.

"Congratulations, *Chief Harris*," she said.

"Hmm, thanks. That has a nice ring to it..."

The detective tried to shift his body but froze, wincing from the pain of the gunshot wound.

"Are you okay?" Samantha asked, moving in closer to the stretcher.

"I'll survive."

Samantha reached out and covered his hand with hers. "I cannot believe this night. And I *really* can't believe Mayor Elliot is in cahoots with Axel Guzman and at the helm of the drug ring. I had a chance to speak with Chief Wentworth while you were inside the house. I've got a lot to catch you up on."

Gregory rested his head against the back of the stretcher and closed his eyes. "I can imagine. Hey, can you do me a favor and check my phone? It's been buzzing like crazy. I don't have the energy to do it myself."

"Of course. Where is it?"

"Inside my coat pocket."

Samantha grabbed the phone and tapped the notifications. "There's a message here from Officer Barris. Ooh! Things are moving fast. It says that Axel Guzman was caught down in the drug lab at Westman's. Both he and Mayor Elliot are currently under arrest, along with Officers Baxter and Miller. Collin's boys are being questioned right now, and they're cooperating with the police."

"That is great news. I still can't believe I left Chicago thinking life would be slower and easier for me here in Gattenburg. Oh, how wrong I was…"

"Yeah, well, at least we're finally getting justice for this town. You should be glad you came and proud of all your hard work. None of this would've been resolved had it not been for you."

"And you."

Samantha tightened her grip on Gregory's hand. "Thank you. After all this, I can't wait to get back to blogging and follow up on this crazy, twisted case. You know what else, Chief Harris?"

"What's up?" he chuckled.

"Tonight just reaffirmed that life is short. I have to go after my dreams. So, with that being said, I've decided to quit my job with the women's journal and focus on my *Someone Knows Something* brand full-time. I'm talking launching a podcast, creating a cold case web series, developing partnerships and sponsorships, the works. I'm about to go global."

Gregory opened his eyes and turned to her. "I think that sounds amazing. You know, what's interesting is that tonight showed me I need to go after what I want, too."

"Oh really? And what is it that you're ready to pursue?"

"You."

Samantha paused, feeling as if everything around her had come to a complete stop.

"What do you think of that?" he asked.

"I think you should go for it…"

Just as the ambulance turned into the hospital's driveway, Gregory wrapped his arm around the small of her back and pulled her in close. He held her chin in his hand and kissed her passionately.

Samantha leaned into him, relishing the feeling of his full, supple lips. She felt every word they hadn't spoken in that kiss. Their shared triumph in solving the Gattenburg murders, how they'd come out of the ordeal unscathed, the love they shared for one another—it was all there.

When the ambulance came to a stop, she gradually pulled away from him.

"Mmm," Gregory sighed. "That was nice."

"Yes, it was," she murmured, her lips still tingling from his touch.

"I'm so glad I don't have to hide my feelings for you anymore."

"So am I. Because it was becoming quite the struggle."

"It was, wasn't it?" he quipped just as the EMTs opened the back door. Gregory took Samantha's hand in his. "You and I have a lot to discuss. And I'm hoping part of that conversation will be about us building a life together."

"It most certainly will."

She watched as the paramedics pulled him from the vehicle. He stared back at her. There was an unspoken, unbreakable bond in their gaze.

And in that moment, Samantha knew that Gregory was the man she would spend the rest of her life with.

* * * * *

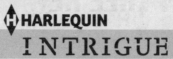
#2013 COLD CASE AT CARDWELL RANCH
Cardwell Ranch: Montana Legacy • by B.J. Daniels

A grisly discovery leads detective Waco Johnson to Cardwell Ranch—and a thirty-year-old unsolved homicide. When evidence points to Ella Cardwell's mother, Waco knows he'll need the rancher's help to find her. But as family secrets are uncovered, Ella and Waco are thrust into a killer's sights.

#2014 DECODING A CRIMINAL
Behavioral Analysis Unit • by Barb Han

Dashiell West's sister is in trouble, and recruiting computer whiz Raina Andress to work with him in cybercrimes at the Behavioral Analysis Unit is his only hope. Raina knows her friend would never embezzle millions, but joining forces with the agent from her past will mean risking her heart again...

#2015 A STRANGER ON HER DOORSTEP
by Julie Miller

The man who collapses at Ava Wallace's door remembers being a Marine, but he has no idea who left him for dead or how he ended up in the mountains of Wyoming. As the stranger begins to recover his memory, every recollection brings them closer to a deadly revelation...

#2016 SEARCHING FOR EVIDENCE
The Saving Kelby Creek Series • by Tyler Anne Snell

When he takes a job to prove himself, fate introduces Deputy Marco Rossi to Bella Greene—a small-town beauty terrorized by a mysterious stalker. As they discover clues leading to the truth, crucial evidence must take priority over the feelings suddenly breaking through his walls.

#2017 A JUDGE'S SECRETS
STEALTH: Shadow Team • by Danica Winters

After her mentor is poisoned and her car is bombed, Judge Natalie DeSalvo knows she's not safe. As she relies upon military contractor Evan Spade to protect her, the search for her assailant leads to shocking secrets, while trusting her heart leads to danger she never imagined.

#2018 AN ABSENCE OF MOTIVE
A Raising the Bar Brief • by Maggie Wells

Attorney Marlee Masters's brother was murdered. Proving it means working with Sheriff Ben Kinsella and facing the nasty gossip in their rural Georgia town. Although the gossips accuse Marlee of being the *real* threat, there's a stalker vowing retribution if the two don't end the investigation.

Get 4 **FREE REWARDS!**

We'll send you 2 FREE Books plus 2 FREE Mystery Gifts.

Harlequin Intrigue books are action-packed stories that will keep you on the edge of your seat. Solve the crime and deliver justice at all costs.

FREE Value Over $20

YES! Please send me 2 FREE Harlequin Intrigue novels and my 2 FREE gifts (gifts are worth about $10 retail). After receiving them, if I don't wish to receive any more books, I can return the shipping statement marked "cancel." If I don't cancel, I will receive 6 brand-new novels every month and be billed just $4.99 each for the regular-print edition or $5.99 each for the larger-print edition in the U.S., or $5.74 each for the regular-print edition or $6.49 each for the larger-print edition in Canada. That's a savings of at least 12% off the cover price! It's quite a bargain! Shipping and handling is just 50¢ per book in the U.S. and $1.25 per book in Canada.* I understand that accepting the 2 free books and gifts places me under no obligation to buy anything. I can always return a shipment and cancel at any time. The free books and gifts are mine to keep no matter what I decide.

Choose one: ☐ **Harlequin Intrigue Regular-Print**
(182/382 HDN GNXC)

☐ **Harlequin Intrigue Larger-Print**
(199/399 HDN GNXC)

Name (please print)

Address   Apt. #

City   State/Province   Zip/Postal Code

Email: Please check this box ☐ if you would like to receive newsletters and promotional emails from Harlequin Enterprises ULC and its affiliates. You can unsubscribe anytime.

Mail to the Harlequin Reader Service:
IN U.S.A.: P.O. Box 1341, Buffalo, NY 14240-8531
IN CANADA: P.O. Box 603, Fort Erie, Ontario L2A 5X3

Want to try 2 free books from another series? Call 1-800-873-8635 or visit www.ReaderService.com.

*Terms and prices subject to change without notice. Prices do not include sales taxes, which will be charged (if applicable) based on your state or country of residence. Canadian residents will be charged applicable taxes. Offer not valid in Quebec. This offer is limited to one order per household. Books received may not be as shown. Not valid for current subscribers to Harlequin Intrigue books. All orders subject to approval. Credit or debit balances in a customer's account(s) may be offset by any other outstanding balance owed by or to the customer. Please allow 4 to 6 weeks for delivery. Offer available while quantities last.

Your Privacy—Your information is being collected by Harlequin Enterprises ULC, operating as Harlequin Reader Service. For a complete summary of the information we collect, how we use this information and to whom it is disclosed, please visit our privacy notice located at corporate.harlequin.com/privacy-notice. From time to time we may also exchange your personal information with reputable third parties. If you wish to opt out of this sharing of your personal information, please visit readerservice.com/consumerschoice or call 1-800-873-8635. **Notice to California Residents**—Under California law, you have specific rights to control and access your data. For more information on these rights and how to exercise them, visit corporate.harlequin.com/california-privacy.

HI21R

Love Harlequin romance?

DISCOVER.

Be the first to find out about promotions, news and exclusive content!

Facebook.com/HarlequinBooks

Twitter.com/HarlequinBooks

Instagram.com/HarlequinBooks

Pinterest.com/HarlequinBooks

ReaderService.com

EXPLORE.

Sign up for the Harlequin e-newsletter and download a free book from any series at
TryHarlequin.com

CONNECT.

Join our Harlequin community to share your thoughts and connect with other romance readers!
Facebook.com/groups/HarlequinConnection